SHIMMERDOGS

SHIMMERDOGS

DIANNE LINDEN

thistledown press

Library and Archives Canada Cataloguing in Publication
Linden, Dianne
Shimmerdogs / Dianne Linden.

ISBN 978-1-897235-37-9

I. Title.
PS8573.I51S44 2008 jC813'.6 C2008-900082-X

Cover photograph ©Anne Domdey/CORBIS
Author photograph: Gary Ford
Cover and book design by Jackie Forrie
Printed and bound in Canada

Thistledown Press Ltd.
633 Main Street
Saskatoon, Saskatchewan, S7H 0J8
www.thistledownpress.com

We acknowledge the support of the Canada Council for the Arts, the Saskatchewan Arts Board, and the Government of Canada through the Book Publishing Industry Development Program for our publishing program.

Acknowledgements

I thank Master Corporal Leanne Karoles for helping me understand her experience as a Canadian peacekeeper in Bosnia from the fall of 2000 to the spring of 2001. And I extend my appreciation to Rev. Britt Jessen, Rena Metheun and her Grade Seven students at Saint Mark's Catholic School, Raffaella Montemurro and her Grade Four students at Virginia Park School, Eva Radford and Dr. Joy-Ruth Mickelson, all of Edmonton, as well as Marg Epp, of Saskatoon, for their insights in viewing successive drafts of the novel. I offer the same to members of the Edmonton CANSCAIP group, particularly Glen Huser, Mary Woodbury, Rita Feutl, Chris Goulet and Gwen Molnar. I greatly appreciate the assistance of Anya S. Zarnoch, who shared her knowledge of Poland and Polish culture with me. And of course I am indebted to Thistledown Press and R. P. MacIntyre for helping this book reach completion.

Thank you all.

For Erika and Tilman, two great kids; for Stefan who is lucky and brave, and for Colonel, who probably did come from the moon and went back there far too soon.

Beginning Times

As soon as I woke up that morning, I knew something strange was going to happen. We were living in Beaumont then, and it was the day where the town dogs get to use the swimming pool. Every year that happens, just before they take the water out of the pool to get it ready for winter. I went to watch with my family because even though we didn't have a dog, I really wanted one.

There were all kinds of them at the pool, with their owners of course. The dogs were very excited. They barked and sniffed each other the way dogs do. A few even wore costumes like little hats or flowers or blankets on their backs.

After a while, a lifeguard-kind-of-person got up on the diving board. "Are you ready?" he shouted.

"Yes!" all the people shouted back. It seemed like they were as excited as the dogs.

"All right then!" he shouted again. He blew a whistle and all the dogs jumped into the water like they knew exactly what to do. The owners called out to them and the dogs barked and churned up the water. I was just standing there watching with Mom, my sister Nellie and my Uncle Martin. I wasn't even that close to the edge of the pool. But someone ran by and bumped into me, and I stumbled backwards, grabbing at things that weren't there. Then the next thing I knew I was in the pool yelling, "Help!" and swallowing more and more water and dog hair until my throat filled up and I went under.

I couldn't see anything except dog paws stirring the water into bubbles that made gurgling noises. Then everything went dark, and after that, I died. It's true. I wouldn't make up a story about something like that.

WHAT I REMEMBER NEXT IS BEING IN a misty place, just standing, standing. Then someone called, "It's time to come back now." At first, I thought it was my mom, except it wasn't her voice calling me. Hers is higher and very clear. This was a tickling voice, kind of like a feather in my ear.

"Don't," I said, because I wasn't used to hearing like that, inside my head I mean, and it made me shiver. Then a dog's face came very close to mine — just a dog's eye, really, which was shiny with lots of colours inside it. The colours twirled around kind of like those things people put outside on their patios, and there was lots of white hair around the eye. I think there was also part of a floppy ear.

I wasn't afraid of the dog though — the part of it I could see, I mean. I closed my eyes and went to sleep.

AFTER A WHILE, I HEARD MY MOM'S voice for sure going, "Son! Come on now." And this time when I looked, it was sunny and I was lying on some grass and she was right beside me. "There you are," she said. Then she looked at my Uncle Martin who was bending down over me so that his face was very red and upside down, with his mouth where his eyes were supposed to be. "I told you he was okay," Mom said to my uncle. "He just got excited and fainted."

Uncle Martin went, "I don't see how you knew that for sure, Alice." That's my mom's name. It's Alice Mackelwain, actually. My sister Nellie and I have Hopkins for a last name, because of the dad we used to have. But Mom loves us anyway.

"How did you know it wasn't cardiac arrest?" Uncle Martin asked her. He straightened up a bit and then I was looking up at his nose hairs. I was surprised they weren't red like his eyebrows or the hair on his head.

"You're forgetting I teach first aid, Martin," Mom said. "I know what to look for."

That's how I got pretty sure I wasn't dead anymore. I don't think you're allowed to argue when you're in heaven.

"Where did the dog go?" I asked. Mom and Uncle Martin looked at each other. He even raised his eyebrows. Then my sister Nellie stepped in between them.

"There are all kinds of dogs here, Mike," she said. "Which one do you mean?"

After she told me about the dogs, I pushed up on my elbows to have a look and she was right! There were dogs all around me in a sort of circle. Their owners were with them of course, but the dogs looked especially interested — except for two of them that were sniffing under each other's tails.

Still, I didn't see the dog I was looking for, so I said, "I mean the white one that followed me after I died."

Uncle Martin blurted, "What?"

I said, "You know — the dog that told me to come back here from that other place."

Mom got a worried look and Nellie said, "He's just confused, aren't you Mikey? You didn't mean to say that." She frowned and nodded at me and kind of pushed my leg.

"Well, yes," I said, "I did mean that! I do! I was dead, and then a dog came and talked to me and told me I had to come back."

"That was Mom," Nellie said.

"No, it wasn't," I said because I can tell the difference between a dog and my own mother! Then I started to cry which is something I'm not supposed to do since I'm the only man Mom and Nellie have. Uncle Martin talked to me about that, but sometimes I forgot.

MOM TOOK ME TO DOCTOR MILLER AFTER I drowned, just to make sure I was okay. It was really Uncle Martin who was worried. He's a teacher in Edmonton, which is close to Beaumont but not close enough for him to come by every day, so he kept phoning and bugging her about it until she finally gave in.

Doctor Miller listened to my heart and hit my knee with a little rubber hammer and did other things. Then he said I was fine. "He's a healthy boy," he said.

"I died, though," I told him.

"Fainted, is what we call it," Dr. Miller said. "Were you afraid in the pool?"

"I hate going in the water," I said, "even at swimming lessons."

"Well then," he told me. "You got scared and fainted for a minute."

When we were leaving, Dr. Miller said to mom, "Your son has quite an imagination, doesn't he?" He was quiet about it but I could still hear what he said because I was really listening.

Mom went, "Oh, yes."

"I don't think it's anything to worry about," Dr. Miller said. "Let him run with it."

"Would there be any way to stop him?" Mom asked, but it didn't seem like a question.

NELLIE FOUND OUT WHAT I SAID TO Dr. Miller and she warned me not to say anything more about what happened at the pool. She told me, "You didn't die, Mike, or you wouldn't be here."

"But it's the truth!" I told her back. "Anyway, I never even mentioned the dog part."

My sister isn't a red head like Mom and me and Uncle Martin, but her face still lights up like ours when she's upset, so she got really rosy then — even white across the nose — and she said, "It's the end of the Twentieth Century. Things like that don't happen anymore — if they ever did." She also told me that my Grade One teacher,

Mr. Charest had phoned Mom to find out if my heart really stopped beating at the swimming pool. Also if it was true that I couldn't take gym anymore because of it.

"Mom is working very hard right now, Nellie said. She has two jobs and she's worried about money, so she doesn't need you making up stories. Also she's unhappy about other things."

"What other things?" I wanted to know.

"Things like us not having a father," Nellie told me. "Stuff like that."

"We have a father," I said. "We just never see him. Plus we don't know where he is."

"It still bothers her," Nellie said. "She thinks you should have some men in your life."

"Well, there's Uncle Martin," I said.

Nellie blew her breath out in a hard little puff. "I think she means a man who isn't weird," she said. "Anyway, it's women's stuff we were talking about. Mom wants to do something important with her life and make a difference. You probably wouldn't understand." After she got in Grade Six, Nellie told me that all the time. "Promise you won't say anything more about dying and coming back to life. Or about talking to trees or anything else like that."

"I never said I could talk to trees," I told her. But she frowned at me so hard that I gave her my promise. And I kept it as long as I could.

I FORGOT TO REMIND NELLIE THAT I HAD another man in my life — Mr. Charest, my Grade One teacher at St. Vidal School. He's the reason I went to a saint's school in the first place even though we didn't go to a church or anything.

Mr. Charest sometimes answered questions if he was in a good mood so one time when it was quiet in the classroom I went up to his desk and asked him, "Do you think people can come back to life after they're dead?" I stayed a little bit away from his desk when I talked because if you get too close, he takes off his glasses to see you better. Then he looks really hard at you, which can make you sweat.

"Besides Lazarus, you mean?" Mr. Charest said. He already told us about a man with that name who came back to life. But Jesus was part of that story, so it wasn't the same.

"I'm talking about today," I said.

"And you're thinking about what happened to you a few days ago at the swimming pool," he said back. I wished he hadn't brought that up. "It's time to let this go, Mike," Mr. Charest told me. "Didn't you go to the doctor about it?" I nodded. "And didn't he say you just fainted?" I had to nod again. "Well then," Mr. Charest said. "That's the end of that."

Then he stood up and said in a loud voice, "Gym time." Everyone in the class but me rushed for the door.

I guess I should be honest and say that Mr. Charest didn't really call me Mike. He always called me by my real name, which is Lester B. — Lester Bowles, actually. It's a dumb name and I don't like it. Most kids with middle names don't get called Rodney G. or Sally V. just because they have them. And Lester is pretty bad, even without the B.

I know I was named for a prime minister who my mom liked because he invented peacekeepers. His name was Lester B. Pearson. But it's a bad name for a kid. Uncle Martin thinks so, too. He told me he started calling me Mike when I was a baby because the first Lester B. had that for a nickname. I'm not sure why. But everyone calls me Mike now, except Mom and sometimes teachers.

That's all I want to say about that subject.

Since I couldn't get Mr. Charest to talk, I decided to visit Mrs. Riley one Saturday to see if she had any books in the library on the subject of dying and coming back to life again. It was pretty much my last idea.

When I got there and I noticed her new, short haircut, I stared my eyes out. "What is it, Mike?" Mrs. Riley asked me. "It's not polite to stare."

Why I was staring is I'd never really seen her ears before and now that I could, I noticed her earrings were just like the eyes of the dog that brought me back to life. But I remembered Nellie's warning, and what I said was, "Your earrings have so many colours in them."

"These?" Mrs. Riley said. She put her hands up to her ears. "They're called opals. People say opals mean death. But I wear these all the time and my ears haven't fallen off yet." Then she laughed and asked me what I was looking for. And of course I couldn't really tell her.

I did find something important on my own, though, just by accident. It was an old-looking book that someone had left out on the table. There weren't any pictures on the cover, but I had a prickly feeling I should pick it up anyway. The title was in gold and it had two parts. First it said, *From the Beginning.* Then it had two dots on top of each other which Mrs. Riley called a colon, then *Dogs through the Ages.*

"This book is too hard for you, Mike," Mrs. Riley told me. "You won't be able to read it without help." Then she gave me the rule about kids not trying to read books that have more hard words on a page than they have fingers on one hand.

And I told her I wasn't worried about fingers. I'd get someone to help me with the reading because I really wanted that book! There was a picture inside that made me know it was a dog that brought me back to life again.

MOM WASN'T JUST A FIRST-AID TEACHER WHEN we lived in Beaumont. She also belonged to the reserve army, and every Saturday she went to Edmonton during the day to learn about using guns and stuff and do something she called parading. The Saturday army isn't for starting wars or killing people. It's for helping them if a volcano blows up or if they're in some other kind of trouble.

Anyway, Mom usually got home late on Saturdays, so we had a pizza picnic together. That means we sat on the living room floor and ate pizza out of the box and drank pop from cans. Mom and Nellie also had carrot and celery sticks but I never did because of not liking things with sharp points in my mouth.

After the pizza we usually watched a movie, but the day I got *Dogs through the Ages*, I asked if we could read it together instead. Nellie didn't want to. She said she had her own stuff to read, so she moved to a chair and Mom and I looked at the book together on the couch. We all had to share the same lamp, because we didn't have that much furniture in the living room.

In *Dogs through the Ages* it told how people and dogs have been together almost since the world began. Some people even say that dogs came to earth from the moon, just after the Creator made people, who were called Two-Leggeds, to help settle them down. The Two-Leggeds were in trouble right from the start because of arguing and starting wars with each other.

When the dogs first got here, they were like shadows, only brighter. They were cold and howled all the time. But the Creator stroked their shivering sides and called them secret names until they warmed up and you couldn't see through them as much. After that the Creator said, "You shall be my holy dogs and you shall teach people to get along and stop fighting with each other." I really liked that part.

Another thing it said in *Dogs through the Ages* is that people used to believe the door they went through when they died was guarded by dogs! The book called it "the door to the after-life." There was a picture with that part. It showed a white dog with eyes like Mrs. Riley's earrings standing beside a door in a cloudy place. I was sure it was the same death place I'd been in.

I felt very excited and wanted to talk to Mom about what we were reading, but Nellie was sitting there so I couldn't. That's one reason I was glad when Merit came. She talked to me as much as I wanted.

I WAS TAKING OUT THE GARBAGE WHEN I saw Merit for the first time. She was in the alley sniffing the garbage cans. I didn't know she was Merit then, of course. And I didn't know she was a girl. I just knew she was a shaggy, white dog who was tall enough that if I bent over a little bit I could look her right in the eye.

Merit wasn't at all shy about looking back. She did it so hard that the bag fell out of my hand and garbage spilled out onto the road. Her eyes were normal then so that's not why it happened. It happened because I felt that feathery voice in my head again. It was even lower and softer this time, kind of like when the radio's on quietly but not tuned in to a station, so I'm not sure exactly what Merit was saying at first. I had to work very hard to understand her.

But I do know that she got right to work helping me clean up the garbage. Mouldy spaghetti and grapefruit peelings and eggshells and coffee grounds and hamburger wrappings — even an old pizza box. Merit helped me with all of it. When we were done, she said, "I came so you'd have someone to talk to."

"Okay," I said and patted her. Then she followed me back to the house.

Nellie had a fit, of course. She said Merit was filthy and probably had fleas. "Anyway," she said, "how do you know she doesn't belong to somebody?"

"She doesn't have tags," I said. "Besides, she told me she's here to stay with me!"

"Mike!" Nellie said in a very cranky way. She stamped her foot. "Don't start that again! And don't you dare say anything like that to Mom!"

So I took Merit into my bedroom and kept her there until Mom got back.

IT SEEMED LIKE MOM WOULD NEVER COME home, but while we were waiting I found out about Merit being a girl. It was an easy thing to do. I just picked up her tail and had a peek underneath it. I kind of knew what to look for.

I thought up Merit's name then, too. It was because of something hanging on the wall in the living room which said, *Certificate of Merit* on it. Then it had Mom's name. She got it before I was born when she saved a boy's life doing CPR. That's when you blow into somebody's mouth to make them breathe because they can't do it for themselves.

I always liked how it made my tongue feel to say *Certificate of Merit.* But I only used the Merit part for the name because of how long it took to say the whole thing. "Here Merit," I said, to try the name out. Then I held out a piece of cracker I found in my pocket and she came right away.

FINALLY I GOT OUT OF THE BEDROOM, and saw Nellie giving our mother a big smile. "You look tired," Nellie said and then she looked at me and made the word *no* with her lips.

But I let Merit out of my room, anyway. "Look who came to live with us," I said. I tried to make my smile bigger than my sister's. "Is it okay?"

Mom sighed, "I'm afraid not." Then I cried just a little bit, and after a while Mom asked, "How do you know she doesn't already belong to somebody?" She looked very sad when she asked me that, like she was going to cry herself.

I said, "She doesn't have tags or anything." Nellie glared at me but I kept on. "Please Mom. She needs a home and she would be very good company when you're not here."

"Oh, brother," Nellie said under her breath. "Get the mop."

"We can't afford to feed her, Lester B.," Mom said.

"She won't eat much," I told her. "And she can have part of my food. I'll even share my cheese pizza on Saturdays." But Mom went on looking sad so I took Merit back into my bedroom and locked the door.

We stayed there a long time until finally Mom said we could try it, but she gave me four rules. First, she said I had to give Merit a bath that very night. Second, we had to put up posters to see if she belonged to anybody. And if she did, we had to give her back without a fuss. Third, Mom said no sleeping with Merit on my bed. And fourth, if there were serious problems she would have to go.

The first two rules were easy. It turned out Merit liked the bathtub. And Nellie helped me with the posters, even if she was mad at me. We put up twenty, but no one came to get her.

It wasn't my fault the third part didn't work so well. Merit wanted to sleep with me. She said it was the best time to talk and I just couldn't get her to stop. And about the fourth rule, well, when Merit went away, it was because she needed to. We didn't ask her to go.

WE GOT MERIT A RED COLLAR AND fastened a dangly silver name tag on it so she wouldn't get lost, because right from the start she did everything with our family. She went out running in the morning with Mom. Then she came home and walked to school with me. At the end of the day, she came back and picked me up again.

And Merit slept with me, even though she wasn't supposed to. Once when we were in bed at night I asked her if she was the same dog who saved my life. She sniffed her paws for a long time like she was thinking with her nose before she answered. I think she actually went to sleep. But when I pushed her with my foot, just gently, she opened her eyes and said, "Well, you're alive again, aren't you?"

BECAUSE OF THE THIRD RULE, MERIT USUALLY stayed under the bed until Mom or Nellie had tucked me in and gone out of the bedroom. But one night after Mom told me good night, she said, "You can come out now, Merit. I know you're under there." Merit crawled out from under the bed with kind of a doggy smile on her face and jumped up with me. "I surrender," Mom said to both of us. Then she gave Merit a pat and went out.

Usually Mom closed the window shade when she was leaving, but that night she forgot. I was getting ready to call her back when Merit looked at me. It was dark, and the light from the street lamp was coming through the window, and I noticed she had little silver moons in her eyes. Not colours, exactly, but still. Moons! That gave me an idea. "You're a moon dog, aren't you?" I said. Merit turned around on the bed a couple of times before she answered. She sniffed her paws like she was thinking with her nose and then she said, "Well, I did have to travel a long time before I got to your house."

That's how I found out that Merit was one of the dogs who helped the Creator, and might be still, so even if she wasn't the exact dog that brought me back to life, I knew she was really special.

WINTER CAME BEFORE WE KNEW IT AND we had Christmas. Then Mom said we could have a special party for New Year's Eve because it was the last time we could use nines to write the date. "Goodbye, 1999," Mr. Charest told us at school. "Hello 2000!" He also said some people thought bad things would happen at midnight, but that we shouldn't worry.

Uncle Martin came to the party, of course. I asked Nellie if he was bringing a girlfriend, and Nellie said, "Uncle Martin? In his dreams." A few of Mom's friends from the Saturday army were there too. One of them was named Lorna Karlsen and she came with her boyfriend. But there weren't any other kids so Merit and I got bored and went to sleep in the bedroom.

A little before midnight, Nellie woke us up. Lorna gave me a little silver paper hat with 2000 on it to wear and a paper horn to toot. We all watched the television and when it was midnight, everyone shouted "Happy New Year!" and made noise. Even Merit barked a few times.

Mom hugged Nellie and me together, and Uncle Martin who doesn't usually do things like that, gave us all a squeeze. Then Mom hugged Lorna, who said, "Maybe I'll see you over there." Mom shook her head in a serious way and looked at me like she was saying, "I don't want to talk about it now."

I had some pop, and a few chips, but things were as boring as before midnight, so Merit and I went back to bed. If the bad things Mr. Charest talked about happened in the world that night, we didn't know about it.

AFTER THE CALENDAR TURNED OVER TO 2000, things just went along and went along and pretty soon it was spring. I really didn't think about death very much anymore, or even about moon dogs. I was just happy, talking to Merit and being normal.

Mom didn't seem very happy, though, and Nellie was cranky almost all the time. I heard them talking together at night after I went to bed and sometimes Nellie got loud or even cried. But I just thought it was more of the women's stuff she'd mentioned before.

Then I found out we were going to Uncle Martin's for a Sunday dinner. That made me worried right away because Uncle Martin is an art teacher and his house is not like ours. His is fancy with stuff all around that you can break if you even look at it. But most of it is so weird you don't want to look at anyway, like the statue of a red heart with spears sticking in it or a picture of a big, bloody eyeball.

Then he has hardwood on the living room floor that's easy to scratch. When we were there last time, Merit ran right onto it as soon as we were inside the house. You could hear her claws going clack, clack, clack. "Not on the hardwood!" Uncle Martin said. "She'll scratch it! Out!" he said to Merit and pointed to the kitchen. Merit just looked at him and lay down.

The other reason I worried about going to Uncle Martin's for dinner is that he's a dangerous cook. It isn't safe to eat hardly anything he makes because of what he sprinkles all over it. But he made me a hotdog that day without any mustard or anything else on it, and without a toasted bun which would hurt the inside of my mouth. I ate the hotdog and used my napkin and didn't slump in my chair. I really tried to be polite, but Nellie just went pick, pick, pick at her food like she was a bird and never even looked up from her plate.

After dinner, Mom said she had something to tell us. She took a big breath and went, "I have the chance to go on a mission to Bosnia for six months. They need peacekeepers there and I'd like very much to be one of them." Everybody was quiet. Nellie kept looking at her plate, Uncle Martin scratched the red hairs on his knuckles, and I didn't really get it so I just sat there. "I'd be on transport," Mom said. "Driving trucks, that is. It would be very safe."

Then Nellie looked up and she said in a rough voice, "You don't know that for sure. There are still land mines everywhere. I've read about them on the internet."

"Nell, please," Mom said. "We've talked about this. The fighting is finished in Bosnia. And I'm going there as a peacekeeper, to build schools and take food to people and help them get back to normal. Not to fight."

"Will you be carrying a gun?" Nellie asked. Her face was all crumpled together and she was twisting her napkin in her hands.

"Yes," Mom said, "all of us will have weapons. But just for self-defence."

"If you need to defend yourselves, then it must be dangerous," Nell said. She even looked at Uncle Martin, but he shook his head and wouldn't talk.

Then Mom went, "It's important work, Nell. You know how we've been talking about making a difference."

"So I guess you're going for sure?" Nellie asked. She threw her napkin down on her plate and stood up. She was glowing like a light bulb. She yelled, "You've made up your mind, haven't you, so what are we even talking about?" Then she ran into the bathroom and slammed the door.

I didn't really know what Bosnia was then. And I couldn't see why Nellie was so upset. But Merit went to the door and started barking like crazy and wouldn't stop, so I had to take her out.

WHEN WE GOT OUTSIDE, MERIT HAD SOME business to do. Then we saw Denver, the black and white dog that lived across the street. We knew him from our other visits to Uncle Martin's.

Denver's owner, Mr. Lapinski, came out of his house just as we were starting across to say hello. Mr. Lapinski was a very old, bent-over person with fuzzy, white hair and thick glasses that made his eyes have rings around them like Saturn. He walked very slowly and used a white cane. "Hallo, Dog Boy!" he called. I hated when he called me that so I pretended I didn't hear him. "Hallo!" he called again, but I put the leash on Merit and tugged a lot to make her come back to Uncle Martin's with me.

NOBODY SAID ANYTHING IN THE CAR ON the way home. Nellie went to her room right away when we got there. But Mom and I talked. Mom told me that Bosnia is a country across the ocean where they had a very bad war with neighbours killing each other. Lots of houses and schools and hospitals were blown up. It sounded just like what happened when the Two-Leggeds were first created.

When Mom said that Canada was sending peacekeepers to help sort out the problems there, I think Merit really perked up her ears. "It's just for six months, remember," Mom said. "I'd leave in September and be back in the spring."

"Who will come and live with us while you're gone?" I asked her.

She said, "I've spoken to your uncle about it. He says you can stay with him at his house in Edmonton."

I was trying not to make a fuss like my sister. I was really trying not to, but I wasn't happy to hear what she was saying. I asked her, "But how will we get to Beaumont every day for school then?"

Mom went, "Oh, well . . . you won't have to. There's a school close to Martin's house you can go to. It's called Mary Chase Elementary School and I think you'll love it."

"Will I have a man teacher?" I wanted to know.

"Well, no," Mom said, "but you wouldn't in Beaumont either for grade two."

I blurted out, "But I don't want to leave Beaumont! I like it here!"

Mom put her hand on my shoulder. "We could try to come back to Beaumont again, Lester B. But I can't promise. Renting this house is very expensive, and I've been thinking we'd have to move, anyway. Maybe when I come back we can find something here that's cheaper."

I did start crying then, but mostly inside my mind. Then Merit came up and pushed her head into my lap, which gave me an awful thought. "What about Merit?" I said. "Will Uncle Martin let her stay with him, too?"

"He'll have to," Mom said. "Merit is part of our family now."

UNCLE MARTIN CAME OUT TO BEAUMONT TO visit us after that. He said he was moving down into the basement so Nellie could have his room and I could have the guest room all to myself. He said he was leaving his computer in the other upstairs bedroom and we could use it to send e-mails to Mom in Bosnia. He even said he'd put away some of his art stuff so it wouldn't get broken. "But Merit has to learn to stay off the hardwood," he said. "You'll just have to train her."

That's how I knew for sure Mom was going. That's how fast things started to happen.

JUST BEFORE WE MOVED INTO UNCLE MARTIN'S house, I woke up in the morning and Merit wasn't there. Mom said not to worry. She said, "Merit was with me when I went for my run. She probably got the scent of a rabbit and went off on an adventure. She'll come back."

But Merit didn't come back. Not that day. Or that night. The next morning Mom, Nellie and I all went out looking for her. Even Uncle Martin came, but it didn't help. Nellie told me, "Everything will be all right," but nothing was. Nellie and I made forty posters and put them up all over town. And we all looked again and again. Merit was gone, though. We didn't find her anywhere.

WE WERE ALREADY STAYING AT UNCLE MARTIN'S and waiting for Mom to leave when a lady phoned us. She lived on a farm around Beaumont and said she'd found a white dog out in the country. It was dead, so she buried it. Then when she went to town she saw our posters. She said she thought maybe the dog was Merit. "It had a red collar, but no nametag," she said. "But tags can fall off and I just wanted to tell you because I know how hard it is to lose a pet."

When Mom mentioned about the lady's call, she said it was good to know Merit wasn't suffering and to go ahead and cry if I needed to. But I didn't need to. I already knew Merit was a moon dog. She'd just gone away on a mission to help settle people down, like Mom was getting ready to do. She'd be back. They both would.

And anyway, Merit couldn't be dead. She would never die without telling me first.

Wars of the Two-Leggeds

AFTER WE MOVED TO UNCLE MARTIN'S, I started waking up a lot more at night because I missed my mom and my Beaumont street lamp. And, of course, I missed Merit. At first I went across the hall when I woke up and tried to get into bed with Nellie. But she didn't like it. She said crabby things like, "Mike, you have your own bed." Once she said, "Mom's gone! Get over it!"

I didn't think that was fair, because I was trying to. I didn't cry at school nearly as much as I wanted to, and I only did it if I had to. My grade two teacher, Mrs. Montcrieff, told me lots of times what a good job I was doing and patted me on the back. I tried to be okay. I even put up pictures of Mom and Merit and me in the guest room to make it feel like mine.

Nellie didn't do anything like that. For a long time, she didn't even unpack her suitcase. She was always sighing and pretending she was reading so she wouldn't have to talk to anybody. I know for sure she was pretending because I watched her and she hardly ever turned a page in her book. She was also very mad about the new school she had to go to, which she called JAWS. She hated it, but it was close to Mary Chase Elementary. Mom and Uncle Martin wanted her to go there so she could pick me up at noon and at the end of the day.

When Nellie did talk, she was very snarky. Then we had fights. Uncle Martin said his hair was falling out in the shower every morning and plugging up the drain because of the way Nellie and I were fighting. He said if we didn't stop, he'd have to call a plumber.

Then we started getting e-mails from Mom and it seemed like she was all right, so I was happier. Even Nellie was, except she was still mad at Mom for going away and never wrote back to her.

Mom told us about the army camp she lived in called Grey Wolf. And she told us how she took food and water to people who needed it. Also about a little boy in an orange jacket, she thought was my age. He followed her van when she went to work fixing up a school near the camp. Mom figured his parents were dead because he was very scared and shy. He only smiled at Mom's roommate, Lorna Karlsen, when she gave him chocolate or orange slices.

EVERY TIME MOM WROTE US SHE SAID we shouldn't worry, that she was safe from dangerous land mines that are buried in the ground and explode when you step on them and kill you, or at least take off your legs. Except Nellie said Mom wasn't really safe because land mines are everywhere in Bosnia and you can walk on one without knowing it. That got me worrying all over again so I made up a little poem to whisper when I was by myself.

I said, "She's on a mission far away, but she'll be back soon one day." I did it that way so I could think about Mom and Merit at the same time. Also to make it rhyme. After we moved into Uncle Martin's, I found out that rhyming things helped me calm down. Sometimes I said the whole poem, but sometimes I just said, "Away, day," over and over again very fast.

It was a lot of work, worrying about both of them and saying the poem so much. It could make me dizzy or tired. But I had to keep saying it because if I didn't, sometimes a shadow zigzagged around in my mind, like it was trying to hurt me. I said the poem faster than ever when the shadow came.

ONE OF THE PROBLEMS AT UNCLE MARTIN'S was I didn't have anything to do after school. Edmonton is too big for me to go around on my own like I did in Beaumont. Also, I didn't have Merit to go with me so what I mostly did when I got home was go over and visit Mr. Lapinski's dog, Denver. I liked him and if I squeezed in my eyes, I could sort of squint out the black spots and make it like I was playing with my own white dog again. We rolled in the leaves and had fun. Sometimes I even called him Merit, and he didn't mind. Once I asked him if he knew where Merit was, but Denver didn't answer. I guess only certain dogs can talk.

I never went over to Denver's house if he wasn't in the yard, though, because then I had to ring the doorbell and talk to Mr. Lapinski. And I didn't like doing that. I didn't like how he stared at me with his scribbled-around glasses and I didn't like the funny way he talked.

I told Nellie I was scared of him and she said I shouldn't be. She said he was just an old man who was going blind. She thought he could still see some kinds of things but not very many.

"What kind of things can he see?" I asked her.

She clicked her tongue and went, "I don't know, Mike. Shiny things like mirrors, maybe. Or big things like trees and busses and hot-air balloons. Go ask him." Nellie's in grade seven now and she's even worse about saying things like that than she was in grade six.

I HAD TO TALK TO MR. LAPINSKI ONE day, though, even if I was scared of him because Nellie said I was driving her crazy. We hadn't heard from Mom for many days and I was worrying and fidgeting and even whispering my poem when Nellie was right there in the room with me. Nellie said, "Stop it, Mikey. Mom told us sometimes they have e-mail problems. It doesn't mean anything."

But I couldn't stop it. I wanted Nellie to phone Mom so I could talk to her and find out if she was all right. Nellie said, "We've tried it before. Don't you remember? They wouldn't let us through because we're kids."

"Well," I said. "I thought you were almost a teenager."

Nellie started to look very red and smudged like she was going to cry. She snapped, "Why can't you get it in your head? Mom's in a war zone full of land mines, and kids don't matter there!"

And I snapped back, "Yes they do! You're just making that up!"

Then Nellie yelled, "You're driving me crazy, Mike! Go visit Denver. Now!" in the kind of voice that hurts my ears.

And I said, “I can’t. He’s not outside.”

“Ring the door bell, then,” Nellie shouted,” and she kind of pushed me out the door.

I decided I’d try it. But I promised myself that if something bad happened, I’d yell, “HELP!” very loud, and I’d yell it over and over until Nellie heard me and felt sorry and let me come back in the house again.

When Mr. Lapinski opened the door, I wasn’t scared, though. I was mad, because he said, “Well, Dog Boy, I wondered when you’d come to visit me.”

“I am not Dog Boy!” I said. I frowned at him very hard so he’d know I was serious. “I’m Mike Hopkins. And I came to visit Denver. My sister told me to.”

“Okay,” Mr. Lapinski said. “Sorry, Mike Hopkins. But you always come with your white dog, so I’m thinking . . . ” He pushed out the glass door on the front of his house and held it open. “Come in. Bring dog, too. Denver will like company.”

“But,” I said, “my dog isn’t here right now. She went away.”

Mr. Lapinski stuck his head out the doorway and turned it to each side like he was trying to see out the corners of his eyes. “Looks like you have dog to me,” he said.

So I looked around behind me because he was acting so funny.

“I don’t see anything,” I said.

Mr. Lapinski said, "No?" He pulled on his chin and it made a scratchy sound. "If you say so, Mike Hopkins." But he didn't push his voice out at me like he usually did. He was quieter and nicer. "But maybe Lapinski sees things you can't."

Then he looked at me — at least I think he was looking at me — and he said, "Come in. Denver is sleeping, but he wakes up for you."

It was kind of like a library in Mr. Lapinski's house, only crowdier. There were books and magazines all along the edges of the room, but in piles, like he wanted them that way. His furniture was old and saggy and Denver was lying on the couch on a folded-up quilt. He opened his eyes when I sat down beside him, and after I petted him a bit, he licked my hand.

Mr. Lapinski said he was going into the kitchen to get me a cookie, and I noticed he kept touching the books as he walked. While he was gone, I opened one of them. It had bigger letters than the books at school and there were funny marks on them. I didn't know any of the words. I couldn't even find "the" or "exit", which were the first words I learned to read.

"You read Polish?" Mr. Lapinski asked me when he came back. "You can borrow, if you like. I used to read them, but now I keep books just for company. And so I know where to walk." He held out a plate with two cookies on it, but I didn't put out my hand to take one.

"Are those black things raisins?" I asked.

"Yes," he said. He sat down in his chair.

"I'm sorry," I said. "I don't eat things with wrinkles in."

Mr. Lapinski smacked himself in the forehead with his hand. Then he looked up at the ceiling and said, "Why I didn't guess?" Then he smiled and showed the gold edges on his teeth. "But you like old men with wrinkles, eh? You like Lapinski?"

"I might be starting to," I said, because he was nicer than I thought — if I didn't look at his glasses too much.

Mr. Lapinski broke the cookie in half. He put one part in his mouth and gave the other part to Denver. "My daughter bakes these cookies. Next time, I ask her to iron wrinkles out."

"Thank you," I said, "but were you joking about seeing my dog?"

Mr. Lapinski leaned forward. "Now I tell you something, Mike Hopkins." Sunlight came through the window and bounced around on his glasses so I couldn't see the rings around his eyes. His mouth looked very straight and serious. "Lapinski may talk too much, but he never jokes about white dogs."

"You don't?" I said. He shook his head. "And you saw Merit for sure?"

He said, "Oh, Lapinski is too old to be sure of anything. Where is your dog, anyway?"

"Well," I said, "she's supposed to be dead." I felt very sad saying the words.

"And you don't believe it." Mr. Lapinski started feeling in his pockets for something, but he didn't find it.

I knew I wasn't supposed to talk about Merit anymore, but it seemed like Mr. Lapinski had seen her, so I just had to tell him what I really thought. I said, "No. I think she's on a mission somewhere, just like my mom. I read about how dogs came from the moon to get people to stop fighting. That's probably what Merit's doing."

"All dogs?" Mr. Lapinski asked me. "Why you didn't tell me this, Denver?" He rocked the dog with his foot. Denver just wagged his tail.

"Maybe not all of them," I said. "But I'm pretty sure about Merit. Except I don't know where she is exactly and I'm getting worried."

"Where you have read about this?" Mr. Lapinski wanted to know. So I told him about *Dogs through the Ages* and how the Creator brought moon dogs down to help her get peace in the world.

"And how you know this Creator was woman?" Mr. Lapinski asked me.

I said, "Because in the pictures she has long braids."

"Maybe it was man with long braids," he said. "Men have long hair. Think about uncle of yours." Mr. Lapinski started a laugh in his stomach that got up into his chest and made him cough. And I laughed too, thinking about Uncle Martin being the Creator with long braids on his head.

When we settled down again Mr. Lapinski said, "I think maybe you are little bit lonely."

"Well." I didn't want to talk about the lonely part because it made my eyes sting, so I said, "Anyway, how can you see things? My sister told me you're going blind."

Mr. Lapinski took off his glasses and his eyes were still there but they were a little crooked. "I can still see out of the sides of my eyes," he said. A little bit." He turned his head. "I can see that you have red hair." And maybe freckles. Or do you need to wash your face?" He winked at me. "But Lapinski also sees things others can't. Always has, long before these eyes got bad. Ever since war."

"How can you do that?"I asked him.

He said, "If I tell you, could be scary story. So you ask uncle if is all right for Lapinski to tell you scary story from war. If he says, 'Yes,' then I will."

I said, "Will your story help me find out more about Merit?"

"I don't know about that," he said.

When I had my coat on and was going to the door, I asked him, "Did you mean to say the war in Bosnia?"

"No," Mr. Lapinski said. "I meant big war. Second big one. It was long ago."

IT WAS TIME FOR SUPPER WHEN I got home. Nellie only ate a little and then she went to her room because it was Uncle Martin's night to do the dishes.

He was still hungry, though. He took a little bottle of mean-looking prickly stuff out of the refrigerator. Nellie says one taste would probably kill a little kid, so I've never tried it, but it really makes him happy. He kept putting it into his mouth with chopsticks until he got sweat on his nose and his upper lip. He said, "Whew!" a couple of times and shook his head.

While he was eating I said, "Mr. Lapinski wants to tell me a story from the war. He says it might be scary." Uncle Martin got up and went to the refrigerator. Then he came back to the table with a different bottle. I asked, "So can he?"

And Uncle Martin went, "Hmmm?" His face was very red and he wiped it with his napkin.

"Can he tell me the story?" I asked again.

"Well," Uncle Martin said, "I think that's up to him."

"That means he can?"

And Uncle Martin said, "Oh, I think Lapinski's harmless enough." Then he pushed back his chair. "If you want, we can get started on your Halloween costume tonight."

"Okay," I said. I was going to be Clifford the Big Red Dog. I thought Merit would like the idea.

I WENT BACK TO MR. LAPINSKI'S THE NEXT day to hear the story. And the day after that and the next day, too. But he wasn't ever home. And Denver wasn't home, either. And I didn't know what to do after that.

I looked and looked for Merit, just in case she was back and Mr. Lapinski had really seen her. I thought she might be hiding, like maybe she was too shy of Uncle Martin because he was crabby about the hardwood floor. I even tried looking out of the corners of my eyes like Mr. Lapinski did, but nothing helped.

Nellie saw me doing that once and she said, "Mike, stop giving me the evil eye."

"I'm not," I said, but she went back to her book before I could even find out what the evil eye was.

I think it was while I was doing my looking that we got a new e-mail from Mom. She said she's gone to visit an old lady who kept her cow chained up because she was afraid it would wander out in the fields and get blown up by a land mine. But Mom said she had three or four dogs and they went wherever they wanted. I thought that was a good sign. It meant the dogs weren't worried about land mines because they already knew where all of them were buried!

It was a whole week, I think, before Mr. Lapinski was home again. Right away I knew something was wrong when a lady opened his front door and said he couldn't have any visitors. Then I heard him calling her and after she went to talk to him, she told me I could come in.

Mr. Lapinski was in his bed and he was very pale, like the squishy bread Uncle Martin never let us eat after we moved in with him. I didn't understand what Mr. Lapinski said to the lady, but she left us alone together.

"Sit, sit," he said. His pyjamas looked crinkly and new and there were lots of pillows piled up behind his back. Also, he had a cross with Jesus on it above his bed.

Mr. Lapinski patted the edge of the bed and I sat down, but farther away, on the end. Then he went, "So, Mike Hopkins."

And that's all.

"Um," I said, because he wasn't talking so I had to. "I came to see you but you weren't home. Where did you go?"

"I just had dizzy spell," he said. "But my daughter was worried, so I stayed with her for few days. She took me to doctor, fed me and made me get fat." He held up his arms but they looked as skinny as ever.

Then he said, "I have surprise for you," and he called out, "Magdalene!" When the lady came in, he asked her, "Could we have those new cookies, please? And milk for my friend, Mike."

The cookies were very smooth this time and they were all exactly the same round shape. I tried one and it felt perfect in my mouth. I even took a sip of the milk to be polite, but I only like cold milk and it was warm so I left the rest.

"I tell you secret," Mr. Lapinski said. "We get these cookies at store. I say to my daughter, Magdalene, Mike Hopkins don't like food that is touched by human hands. Am I right?"

"Maybe," I said. But I didn't want to talk about food. I wanted to know about the war. And I wanted to know how come he could see a white dog when he was supposed to be blind, but I couldn't, even though I didn't need glasses. I said all that really fast.

"Whew! Slow down," Mr. Lapinski said. "You make air hot." He fanned at his face with his hands. That made the white hair on his head kind of move up and down. But he had lots of white hairs on his chest that showed at the top of his pyjamas, and they didn't move at all.

"Please," I said.

Mr. Lapinski went, "This is serious talk?" I nodded. "Uncle says it's okay?" I nodded again. "Close door, then," he whispered. "If Magdalene hears, she thinks her father is . . . " He made a circle in the air around his ear.

I closed the door and sat back down and waited. I decided to look right at Mr. Lapinski's glasses so he'd know I was interested. It didn't hurt me at all.

"When I was young," he said, "thirteen, I think, there was bad war. You know about that. Your mother is soldier." I nodded. "Then my brave Poland was invaded by soldiers from another country."

I didn't know what that meant. He told me, "Invaded means they came into our country and took away our freedom. You understand freedom?"

"Everybody understands about that," I said. "It means you can do anything you want."

Mr. Lapinski went, "Not anything, but I know what you mean." He told me freedom was especially important to Poles, who were people in Poland and not like things you put in the ground. He said everyone fought the soldiers, but especially the boys in his village. They had to because all the men were gone to Poland's army.

He said, "We didn't have many guns, but we went out at night and bothered soldiers. We took down bridges they needed and burned their trucks. Then they found out where we lived in hills of south and they came to get us. When we looked down and saw them on road, my mother sent me and my brother away to hide."

Mr. Lapinski said his brother's name was Marek — that's Mark in English — and he was only eleven. He said their mother told them to go to a faraway cave that was high above the village. She said the soldiers would track the boys down with their dogs if they stayed close. She told them, "You stay there. Don't you move. When soldiers are gone, I'll come to get you."

Mr. Lapinski was just Nellie's age in the story. It made me sad to think about her going away with soldiers and dogs chasing her. I thought dogs were good, so I didn't see why they would do that.

I think it made him sad too because he said, "Give me your milk," in kind of a rough voice, and his hand was shaking when he took the glass. After he had a big drink, he gave the glass back to me and said, "So we went away and hid for many days, but no one came for us. We ran out of food and we were cold. Then snow and wind came. It was real storm. Devil weather. Marek got fever, so I took off jacket and put on him to keep him warm and I wrapped my arms around him."

Mr. Lapinski was swallowing and looking very sad. "I don't talk about this for many years," he said. "Words are hard to say."

"It's okay," I told him. I moved up the bed a bit. I was trying to get up my nerve to pat his hand, the way Mom always did when I was upset, but I felt shy to do it.

Mr. Lapinski said, "One night I was holding Marek and shivering hard because after dark it got very cold. Then I had feeling someone was watching us, so I looked up. Wind was blowing snow everywhere so was hard to see, but I thought I saw white wolf at front of cave. And it was big, like from old story. I was sure we would die and I said prayers."

I whispered, "Oh, no," and I moved a little closer. Mr. Lapinski took hold of my wrist.

"It wasn't wolf though, Mike Hopkins. Thank God for that." Mr. Lapinski took two fingers and touched his forehead, his chest and both shoulders with them. We did that every day at St. Vidal School with Mr. Charest. It's called making the sign of the cross.

Mr. Lapinski went, "It was white dog. And dog came over to us and I thought it whispered, 'You are safe.' Only in Polish. 'You are safe. Mother will find you.' Then dog got down and curled around us and we were warm and not afraid and we slept until mother came, just like dog said."

"Was the dog still there?" I wanted to know.

Mr. Lapinski shook his head. "Gone." His eyes were closed after that and it seemed like he went to sleep. I touched the top of his hand with my pointing finger, just gently where a springy blue vein stood up.

"You can call me Dog Boy, if you want to," I said. "I'm getting used to it."

⚡

I WENT BACK TO SEE MR. LAPINSKI AGAIN the next day, but his daughter said he was sleeping. "Come back tomorrow," she said, "He'll be glad to have your company."

So I did what she told me and this time Mr. Lapinski answered the door himself.

The bathrobe he was wearing looked as new as his pyjamas. And he had shiny new slippers on his feet. "You like new clothes?" he asked. "One good thing about having little sick spell. You get new nightclothes. Old man like me — usually I just sleep in underwear." That made me laugh because we don't usually talk about underwear in my family.

After we were finished milk and cookies — at least I finished the cookie part and Mr. Lapinski had the rest

— he sat in his chair and I sat on the couch with Denver. I said, "Could you please tell me about what happened when you woke up?"

"Today, you mean?" he asked. He scratched his head and then he winked.

"No," I said. "The day your mom came to find you and your brother. In Poland, I mean.

Mr. Lapinski shrugged his shoulders. "Mother cried. I cried. And then she said it was miracle."

"What was?" I asked.

"Well, we looked all around for paw prints in mud and there weren't any. Only our footprints. And in spot where I first saw dog?" Mr. Lapinski stopped talking and turned his head over his shoulder.

"Yes?" I said, and leaned forward.

"In spot where I first saw dog, water bubbled out of rocks. It was clean and sweet and we drank some of it."

"And that's what you call a miracle?" I asked. "Water coming out of rocks?"

He nodded. "Well, sure, "he said. "Lapinski couldn't make it happen. Could you?"

"Of course, not," I said. "But I thought a miracle was like . . . nothing can save you and then something does."

Mr. Lapinski nodded again. "Could be. Maybe you need sign that this Creator of yours with long braids is taking care of you." My eyes went stinging again but I still told him how the dog brought me back to life after I was drowned. "Do you think that was a miracle, too?"

Mr. Lapinski pushed up out of his chair and gave his arms a little stretch. Then he walked over and rested his fingers on the top of my head. "I think you are lucky boy, Mike Hopkins," he said. "I'm proud of you."

"About the miracle?" I asked.

Mr. Lapinski gave me the kind of smile that showed his gold fillings again and he said, "I think . . . miracle is very deep subject. Too deep for old man wearing new bathrobe."

AFTER I HEARD MR. LAPINSKI'S STORY, A whole bunch of new questions came into my head. But he wouldn't give me the answers so I wanted to check in *Dogs through the Ages* again. Mrs. Montcrieff looked for me on her computer and they didn't have it in any of the Edmonton libraries. Then I tried to get Uncle Martin to take me to Beaumont on Saturday. He said he couldn't. "There's a lot going on this week, Mike," he said. Which meant he didn't want to.

So I decided to ask Nellie to take me on the bus. "Why do you need to go to Beaumont?" she said. She was making microwave popcorn which was our favourite snack for after school.

"I need to check out *Dogs through the Ages* again," I said.

"What for?" she asked me. "You've already read every word in it a hundred times."

"Of course I have," I said. "But I think I might have missed something."

"Like what?" Nellie wanted to know. I just shrugged and watched while she tore open the popcorn bag and a little puff of steam came out. I couldn't say anything because if I didn't know what I missed, how could I say what it was? "I need to go, though," I said, "so could you take me?"

Nellie went, "No, I couldn't. It would take a whole day to get there and back." She put some popcorn in a bowl for her and shoved the rest of the bag at me. "But I can tell you something I don't think you know." She chewed on a couple of popcorn kernels while I watched. "If you look carefully through a telescope, you'll see that the circles on the moon's face aren't really holes. They're little, round doghouses. Check it out some time. There are still dogs living up there."

"Really?" I asked her. "Is that the truth?"

Nellie grabbed her bowl and started to go in the bathroom. "Of course it isn't, Mike! Where's your brain?

It was just a story." I tried to follow her but she shut the door and locked it.

"Stories can be true!" I shouted. I was thinking about the one Mr. Lapinski told me.

"Not stories about dogs who come from the moon and bring people back to life," Nellie shouted back." I gave the door a kick — just a little one. Then Uncle Martin came home.

ONE WAY UNCLE MARTIN AND MOM ARE the same is they both hate it when we fight. He gets big creases in his forehead and presses his lips together so they get really white. He told Nellie to come out of the bathroom. Then he told me to go in and take a hot bath and calm down. He used a very loud voice both times.

Except I didn't want to touch the long, red hairs in the tub or see them floating around, so I just let the water run down the drain. Then I sat on the toilet and repeated my poem forward and backward, lots of times each way. It felt good and it made the shadow in my head stop zigzagging and settle down. I went on saying it and saying it. I had a hard time to stop.

I THINK IT WAS THAT NIGHT WHEN I got up to go to the bathroom and heard Uncle Martin talking on the phone. He said, "Alice doesn't want the kids to know how bad the land mine problem in Bosnia is, but she says there are so many it will take a miracle to get rid of them all in thirty years."

That was very bad news. Even if I was in Grade Two then, I was good enough in math to know that thirty years is a really long time!

THE NEXT DAY WAS HALLOWEEN. I DIDN'T have much time to think about what Uncle Martin said on the telephone because I was busy all day. First, I had school in the morning. Then I put my costume on at noon and wore it all the rest of the day. I liked being Clifford and there wasn't even a tiny piece of shadow in my mind all afternoon. I barked at little kids and howled and ran around. Sometimes it almost felt like Merit was running beside me. Once I even thought I saw the end of her white tail going into the boys' bathroom at school, but only a kid in Grade Six was there when I went to look.

"What are you staring at?" he said. So I went out again.

⚡

NELLIE WAS FEELING SICK SO UNCLE MARTIN took me out trick or treating. It was very magic, with people crunching through the leaves in their costumes and waving their flashlights around. Uncle Martin started telling me things. "You know, Mike," he said. "This makes me think of the first Halloween your mom and I spent in Edmonton. I was about your age. I dressed up like a Roman soldier. Your mom was a gypsy and we were upset because it was cold and we had to put snowsuits on over our costumes. We used to call out 'Halloween apples!' instead of saying, 'Trick or treat!'" You could get apples from people then, he said, or homemade cookies and you didn't have to worry if they had razor blades in them or not.

When we got home, Uncle Martin had to check if he left some schoolbooks in his car and while I was waiting for him by the back door, I heard a voice kind of like Merit's say my name. It was right in my ear, and I jumped and turned around so fast I spilled some candies from the orange pumpkin pail I was carrying them in. "Merit?" I said. I couldn't see anything white. Then I heard the voice again. I thought it said, "To get a miracle, find a sign."

I jumped another time and went, "Where are you?"

Someone said, "Over here," in a loud whisper, but it wasn't Merit. It was Uncle Martin.

"I wasn't talking to you," I said, because I knew Merit would never come out if she saw him. "I was just talking . . . "

"To yourself," Uncle Martin said. "When you start answering we're going to get worried." Then he put his hand on my shoulder and we went inside, but I felt something brush against my leg just before we closed the door.

I WASN'T SURE WHAT KIND OF SIGN I was supposed to find. If it would be something small like the refrigerator door opening all by itself and all Uncle Martin's little bottles lighting up. Or special writing coming in front of the picture on the TV. Or if it would be a big sign, like I'd wake up one morning and a hundred dogs would be sitting out on the front lawn waiting to talk to me.

Then we got two really important e-mails from Mom and I found out I was right to look for something big because there *were* a hundred dogs all right, but not in

Uncle Martin's front yard. They were in Bosnia, helping to find land mines. I don't know how they learned to do it, but there they were!

Mom only knew two of the dogs, who were German Shepherds, not white ones, and their names were Sherlock and Watson. She said they had such good noses that if you filled up the bathtub and then put one drop of blood in it, they could smell it there. So how Sherlock and Watson and the others find the mines is they smell stuff leaking out of them into the ground. Then they show people where they are so they can get rid of them.

The second e-mail was so amazing that I memorized part of it to keep it in my mind. Mom started out telling us that she found out the name of the boy with the orange jacket. She said it was Edin. His parents were dead, like she thought, but he had a sister who took care of him, and an older brother named Mirsad.

Then this is the part I learned by heart. "We've noticed there's a white dog following Edin around. It hides away from us, but it's always near him. Lorna calls the dog 'Edin's Angel'. She says she's seen it tug on his sleeve to keep him from wandering off the road where it isn't safe to walk. I thought you'd like to know."

I WAS HAPPY TO FIND OUT MERIT AND the other dogs were in Bosnia. I thought maybe they didn't need a miracle anymore, but I kept looking for other signs, just in case. I tried different ways of doing it. Sometimes I opened my eyes really wide, and sometimes I squinted out of my eye-corners like Mr. Lapinski. Except when Nellie was around I didn't, because of the evil eye. I never really saw anything you could call a sign, but I did see a lot of things I never noticed before.

Like, I saw that a rabbit was sleeping under the spruce tree in front of the house and eating Uncle Martin's fancy grass that he bought from the garden store. When it was resting, it looked like a big cat because it kept its long ears folded down over its back and it licked its paws and then wiped its face with them. But when it got up, its ears were high on its head. Also, the rabbit was starting to turn white because of winter coming.

And I noticed that Mr. Lapinski's thumbs were very wide and round on the ends, kind of like spoons. And there were big freckles on his hands with interesting shapes. He told me one of them looks like a map of Poland.

Also I saw that when a new friend of ours named Christine came to visit, Uncle Martin fussed a lot about cleaning up and when she said, "Oh, Martin," in a voice that sounded like blowing into a coke bottle, he got as red as one of those Christmas flowers.

I didn't mind sharing Christine, but she was my friend first. How I knew her was the teachers got her to come to school and pretend to be a dead artist — a lady painter we were studying named Emily Carr. Christine walked in the halls with her paints in a baby carriage and a stuffed monkey on her shoulder. It was like a play except we could talk to her and ask questions and she answered back in a funny accent. I was getting ready to ask her how come she could be dead and still visiting our school, when this girl asked her, "Have you seen my grandmother? She just died."

Then Christine said, "Oh, I think she's up in heaven with Alice."

Well, my mother's name is Alice. She's Master Corporal Alice S. Mackelwain, so I thought she was the one who was dead and I cried a lot and couldn't stop. Uncle Martin was on a field trip so Nellie got called to the school. Then she was kind of mad at me.

Anyway, Christine phoned Uncle Martin at home to apologize and see if I was all right. She called me Lester B. then because of meeting me at school. But she got over it. You could see that Uncle Martin wasn't going to get over her, though. He went weirder than ever after that. He sang goofy songs in the shower and even bought himself some new clothes. "Give me a break," is what Nellie had to say about that.

⚡

There's one other thing I noticed when I was trying to find signs. Nellie was still kind of crabby, but she was mostly tired and sad. She didn't grump or snap much any more. Usually if I came up behind her while she was reading and grabbed her book away she got mad and said things like "Beat it, Mike!" and then she chased me. But when I did that after Halloween, she just said, "Whatever," and looked off into space.

I decided she was acting like that because she had a secret — not a good one though, because of how unhappy it was making her.

⚡

After I read Mom's e-mail about the kids at the school in Bosnia needing books, I saw how many I had that I didn't need. And I thought other kids might have books they didn't need, too, so I talked to Mrs. Montcrieff about if we could collect books to send to Bosnia. She said, "Yes."

Pretty soon, our classroom was full of books and pencils, erasers and little notebooks, and even coats and mitts — things like that. Most of us wrote letters to Edin. I even got to buy him a pair of boots because Mom said he only had sandals and thin socks. "Find something that fits you," she said, "and I'm sure they'll fit him because he's just your size."

Then Mrs. Montcrieff told us that the mayor of Edmonton, who's like the boss of the whole city, decided to come to our school on Remembrance Day and give my class an award for our collecting. He was going to Bosnia himself because of all the Edmonton soldiers who were there.

But I still had a problem. My sister was getting sadder and sadder. Sometimes she didn't talk at all. I went into her room without knocking one night, which usually makes her really mad, and she didn't even say a word. She just sat there and held a lighted candle.

"Why are you doing that?" I asked her. I thought it would bother her that I was snooping. Then if she got mad at me, I'd know she was okay.

But she just went, "I'm thinking." And when I asked her what she was thinking about, she said, "I'm thinking about how all kids should be safe, no matter where they live." Then she blew out the candle and sat there in the dark.

FINALLY, NELLIE TOLD US SHE REALLY DID have a secret. And I was right. It was a bad one. Uncle Martin found a note someone gave her at school. It said, "I'm going to kill you, Nellie the Mouse." It came from a boy named Shane who was calling her bad names and doing things he wasn't supposed to like looking down her shirt. Also his girl friend who was called Bonnie said she was going to beat Nellie up.

Uncle Martin got very upset when he heard about it. He pressed his lips together like he always does and said they had to see the principal at Nellie's school. Then Nellie got upset back and said, "Why don't you just shoot me?" That's what she said.

She was crying and acting very afraid and that made me want to do something, but I didn't know what to do except keep saying my poem over and over again. I did it a hundred times every night before I went to sleep because that's how many dogs there were in Bosnia getting rid of land mines. And if I got mixed up on my counting, I started over again.

THEN IT GOT TO BE TIME FOR our Remembrance Day assembly with the mayor. We had it on Friday morning because Remembrance Day was on Saturday and we wouldn't be at school. Mrs. Montcrieff told us we could invite anyone we wanted, but Uncle Martin had to work. And Christine did too. She was being a dead person at another school that day. Mr. Lapinski said, "No thank you. I told you war story. Now Lapinski don't want to think about those times any more."

Nellie came though. She was feeling better because the principal at her school told Shane and his girlfriend Bonnie they had to behave. He even kicked Bonnie out of school for a while.

It was a good assembly. We had bagpipes to start and a peacekeeper marched in who was dressed just like my mom. Then the mayor gave my class a piece of paper with all our names on it in fancy writing. It also had the date, November 10, 2000 and a gold, shiny circle. He said we got it because we were all very good citizens.

After that, the peacekeeper talked to us about the things he did when he was in Bosnia. People were still fighting then and he walked around with a gun and tried to calm then down. He said keeping peace is very hard work and we should all try it. I don't know if he meant without the guns.

Then after we had a minute's silence, Mrs. Montcrieff got up and told how Remembrance Day is about remembering people who died in wars, but it's also about why we shouldn't have wars anymore.

And I forgot to say the librarian and some older kids helped me make a Power Point show for the assembly. We found pictures of two mine-sniffing dogs on a website and put them in. People clapped and said it was good.

But the rest of the day wasn't good because of what Bonnie and her friends did to my sister while we were on our way home for lunch. I don't know what you call a day like that.

SOMETIMES WHEN WE WERE WALKING HOME AFTER school, Nellie played shadow tag with me. She did in the Beaumont days at least, but never at lunch because then we had to hurry. After the assembly, I asked if we could play again because of how well things went and Nellie said, "Sure. If you can find your shadow I'll play with you."

But then I couldn't; only a tiny, stumpy one and that made me grab Nellie's hand because I thought it might mean something

"It's because of the sun, Mikey," she said. "We never get long shadows this time of day. Haven't you noticed that before?" But she laughed when she said it and didn't let go of my hand.

"Okay," I said. "Let's chase each other." I was just starting to run when I tripped and fell on the ground and right by my foot was a little white rock that looked like a dog's head. You could see the nose and the ears kind of standing up. I forgot Nellie didn't want to hear about my dogs and I said, "Look, Nellie! I think this might be from Merit! It's a sign for sure!"

But Nellie didn't hear me. She was standing very still, looking down the street. Then I looked too and there were some girls whistling and running our way. That's when I heard the breathing. It was very quiet but I heard it anyway, like a dog panting.

"Mikey," Nellie said. She bent over and looked right at me. "It's Shane's girlfriend and there's going to be trouble. I want you to go home. Get the key from under the doormat. Then go inside and wait for me."

I got up and put the rock in my jean jacket pocket. Then I spitted on my hands where the gravel made them bleed and rubbed them on my jeans. "No," I said. "I'm not leaving." I said that because Nellie looked really scared and the girls were getting closer. And because she's my sister and I'm supposed to look after her. Also, the breathing sound kept getting louder and louder, like whoever was doing it was really close, and the air was getting doggy smelling and I couldn't move anyway because I felt dizzy.

Then Nellie said, "Mike!" in a bossy voice. She turned me around and gave me a big push. "March!" Just when she said that, I felt something tugging my coat sleeve and pulling me along. I looked and it wasn't like anything I imagined before. It was sort of a dog — or just a dog shape, really. It shined, and faded in and out. And it had jewellery eyes that looked right at me.

My stomach went funny but I tried to be brave. Inside my head a voice said, "Run with me," so I did. I ran faster than I ever have. It was like flying. I followed the dog right up to the front door of a house with a neighbourhood parent sign in the window. Then I rang the doorbell.

The man who opened the door was wearing a uniform like a policeman. "HELP," I said. Even though I was very out of breath, I got out what I wanted to say. "HELP! POLICE! Some girls are trying to kill my sister!"

THE MAN IN THE UNIFORM WASN'T REALLY a policeman. His name was Mr. Vernon and he was a security guard. He was just going to work, but he ran back with me and when we got to Nellie, she was lying on the ground. It made me cry to see her eye bleeding and getting swollen. But I didn't cry very much, because she was saying mixed up things, like she thought she was in Bosnia. And she thought Mr. Vernon was a peacekeeper, so she needed me to be grown-up and talk to her.

I got down and put my face next to hers. I tried to speak clearly so she'd understand. "This isn't Bos-ni-a," I said. "It's Ed-mon-ton. And the man's not a peace-keeper. He's a se-cur-i-ty guard."

I looked around to see if the dog was still there. But it was gone. I was starting to be used to stuff like that.

Mr. Vernon said my sister had to go see the doctor right away. He looked worried when he said it. He told me, "I'll take her in my car, but you need to stay with my wife until someone can pick you up." Then he asked me for my parents' names.

"It's my uncle," I said. "I don't have parents. Just my mom, and she's in Bosnia." Then I gave him the name of Uncle Martin's school.

After we got Nellie in the car, we drove to Mr. Vernon's house and he let me out.

"Tell my wife you're to stay until your uncle picks you up," he said. "Oh, and she's giving violin lessons to senior citizens today so you'll have to read quietly or do your homework."

"We don't get homework in Grade Two," I said. But he was already driving away.

I STOOD OUTSIDE MR. VERNON'S HOUSE FOR A while. I was deciding if I would go in or if I'd go to Mr. Lapinski's house. Then Mrs. Vernon came out the door. She looked kind of like Mrs. Riley, at the library in Beaumont, but she was thinner and smelled like cough drops. I really didn't want to go inside with her, but she said how she was a registered block parent and I would be safe with her. "You really must stay here until your parents get home," she said. "That's what the police want you to do." I already told her husband about my parents so I didn't do it again.

She showed me where I could sit and she brought me a sandwich and some milk. Then an old man came in with a little black case and they went away to another room. In a minute, awful screeching sounds started coming out.

I looked at the sandwich. It had crusts on it. Also, the milk wasn't very cold and I wasn't hungry anyway. But I was sad. I started thinking about all the sandwiches Nellie made for me with interesting shapes and I knew I had a big shadow coming. I could feel it pushing up behind my nose and squeezing on my throat. Then my jaw started shaking and made my teeth click together.

I didn't like the sound my teeth made, especially with the violin screeching up and down, but I tried to sit hard on the chair and hold on to everything because Mrs. Vernon said the police were expecting me to stay. Except I felt worse and worse so I grabbed my Clifford backpack and ran out the door. I kept on running until I got to Mr. Lapinski's.

The partly invisible dog wasn't anywhere around, but I pretended it was. I pressed on the rock in my pocket so I could run faster. And I barked and yelped as loud as I could to push all the shadows out of me. When I got to Mr. Lapinski's house, I was just whimpering and crying and I was almost a boy again.

I rang the doorbell like this — one short push, one long push and then one short push again. It was supposed to be a signal, so Mr. Lapinski would know it was me and that it was very important. But I had to give the signal two or three times.

Finally he opened the door. His hair was standing up at the back like he'd been in a big wind and his shirt was buttoned up wrong. "Dog Boy!" he said "Why you are leaning on doorbell like that?" Then he looked at his watch. "And why you are not in school?"

"I was," I said. I talked fast like my mouth was still running. "We had our Remembrance Day assembly. But my sister almost got killed, except that a sort of dog thing helped me save her. I don't know what it was. First I went to the security guard's house. Mr. Vernon's. But his wife was giving violin lessons, which hurt my ears, and now I need someplace to stay. Can I come in? May I?"

"Sure," Mr. Lapinski said. He opened the door. "Of course you come in."

I went into his living room and everything in it seemed different from the last time. The newspapers were whiter, and Mr. Lapinski's chair was brighter. Denver even looked younger and more wide-awake. So I thought, "They already know about what happened. They already found out."

I ate lots of cookies at Mr. Lapinski's. I also ate a piece of cheese. But I didn't drink hot milk, even when he begged me. "Just this once," Mr. Lapinski said. "I always had warm milk when I was boy. It's good for shock." But I still wouldn't. I didn't want to see the little skin that gets on the top.

For a while I was shivering, but Mr. Lapinski gave me a blanket to wrap up in. After that, I told him everything that happened. He acted surprised, like he didn't know about it after all. But he did know who the security guard was because he's lived here a long time and knows everybody. He called Mrs. Vernon and said where I was. He even called my house and left a message for Uncle Martin because he wasn't at school any more.

Then I asked him, "Who do you think it was that helped me save Nellie? It looked like a dog, but I could see right through it."

Mr. Lapinski looked very grey sitting in his chair. He shook his head. "I don't know, Mike," he said.

I said, "But you told me about . . . "

Mr. Lapinski held up his hand for me to stop. "Lapinski says too much. Tells too many stories."

"I have to know," I said. I was getting really upset. "Please tell me."

He tapped the ends of his crooked fingers together and was quiet. Then he whispered, "Maybe it was spirit that helped you."

"A spirit?" I asked him. "Like a ghost, you mean?" I shivered, because when stuff like that happens for real, it isn't like reading about it in a book or making it up.

"You could say ghost. For me is spirit. They are always around."

I said, "I don't really like to think about ghosts. How they live in your house and try to suck your blood at night."

"Vampires," Mr. Lapinski said. "They're the ones that suck blood, if you believe that." He got up to get a glass of water. He was moving very slowly with one hand on his back and I heard his knees creak. "But spirits can be good. When you came over to my house for first time, I saw one with you then. A shimmerdog. Remember?"

That's when the idea came into my head that maybe Merit was dead after all, like everyone thought. That maybe it was her ghost I saw. And what Mr. Lapinski saw when I first came to visit him.

Then I thought about the lady calling and saying she'd buried a dead, white dog. I didn't want Merit to be dead and buried in the ground even if her ghost was good and helpful. I didn't want my sister to be dead, either. Or people in Bosnia, like Edin or his brother or sister. And especially not my mom! When I thought about that, my jaw started shaking again and I cried very loud.

"There's room for two in this chair," Mr. Lapinski said. So I went and sat next to him. I cried so much I had to blow my nose on his big red handkerchief. Then my eyes started to close and I heard him say, "War is very hard on young boys." Then he went, "Sleep now," and he said some other words I didn't understand, but at the end I thought he called me Merit.

Nellie was already in bed when I got home to Uncle Martin's. She was lying on her side and she didn't move when I went in the room. Her eye was swollen and blue and red. Uncle Martin said she also had very sore ribs and her ankle was hurt and all wrapped up.

"Nellie," I said.

Uncle Martin butted in, "Mike. Don't wake her up. She's had a terrible shock and she needs to rest."

"But I'm afraid she's going to be dead," I told Uncle Martin and my face got wet again.

"She isn't," he said. "They gave her pills to help with the pain and it's made her sleepy. Now let's leave her alone."

But I didn't think Nellie should be by herself so I sat in a chair beside the bed. I stayed a long time. Once she rolled over and opened her eyes. "Please, Nellie, don't die," I said. "Mom will be upset if you do."

But Nellie closed her eyes again, so I don't know if she heard me. Then Uncle Martin came back into the bedroom. "Mike," he said. "This is getting ridiculous. Your sister is not going to die. Now come and have some supper." He lifted me out of the chair and I let him because I was really tired.

NELLIE HAD TO STAY HOME FOR A while until she healed up. At first she was mad and scared and said she wouldn't ever go back to JAWS. But then she and Mom talked a lot on the phone and sent e-mails to each other. And Christine came, too, and talked to Nellie. Plus, she got cards from kids in her class she thought hated her. Her friend Sam brought them. He got his dad to drive him to Uncle Martin's in his taxicab. Even the principal came to visit. He brought my sister a rose and asked her please to come back to JAWS and help make things better. She decided she'd try it until Christmas.

And I decided something, too. I decided I'd be patient for Mom to come home to visit us for the holidays. It wasn't easy, especially after we mailed all the books and pencils and letters to Bosnia. *And* all the stuff for Edin.

Nellie gave me a calendar to mark off the days until Mom came home. I put an X on it every morning when I got up. Then I tapped all around it, to make sure the X did its job.

A FEW DAYS BEFORE MOM GOT HOME, MR. Lapinski asked me if I saw the shimmerdog again. I told him I didn't, but I kind of wished I did, to find out if it was Merit's ghost or not. I also kind of wished I wouldn't see it, because of not wanting Merit to be dead. Then I asked, "Are you sure that's what I saw?"

Mr. Lapinski shook his head. He said, "Is tricky world, Mike Hopkins. Very tricky. Hard to know what things really are."

He was right about that.

The Tricky World

UNCLE MARTIN DROVE US TO THE AIRPORT to pick up Mom. His car is green with very soft covers that give you electric shocks when you slide across them. I sat in the back seat with Nellie because Uncle Martin read it was safer.

Nellie was feeling pretty good again. Teachers at her school had a special way for kids to buy Christmas candy canes and get them delivered to their friends, and Nellie got ten!

"It will be good to see your mom," Uncle Martin said. He was humming and tapping his hands on the steering wheel while he drove. We could see his smiling eyes in the mirror. They were smiling a lot by then. He said, "I'm sorry Christine couldn't come with us today. I want Alice to meet her."

Uncle Martin never would say if Christine was his girlfriend or not and I asked him lots of times. So I decided to try another way. "Uncle Martin," I said. Nellie shook her head right away like she could see into my brain and tell what I was going to say.

Uncle Martin said, “Yes?” and kept on humming and tapping.

“Are you and Christine getting married?”

“Mike,” Nellie said under her breath. Uncle Martin gave a quick look over his shoulder. “Is this a serious question?” he asked me.

“Yes,” I said. Nellie thumped me on the arm and frowned at me.

He stopped tapping and I think the tips of his ears went red, but he said, “We are getting to be quite close.”

”Like you’re kissing and all that stuff?” I asked.

“Mike!” Nellie hissed at me again.

“Well.” Uncle Martin said. He kind of blew out his lips and I think he was going to answer but then Nellie butted in.

“Uncle Martin, what are you fixing for Christmas dinner? Chinese, I hope.” She used her nicest voice, but I could tell she was faking. She never wanted to talk about cooking.

“Chinese food?” Uncle Martin said. “For Christmas?”

I was just getting ready to say something when Nellie butted in another time. “Will we have turkey?”

Uncle Martin started tapping on the steering wheel again. “You know, I thought we’d have something English like roast beef and pudding since Christine is eating with us.”

"Except she's from Scotland," Nellie said, and smirked.

Uncle Martin jerked his head around to look at her for just a second. "How do you know that?" he said.

"When I was home from school," Nellie said. "We talked and she told me."

Uncle Martin sniffed, "Well. She sounds English to me."

Nellie said she hoped he wasn't going to make some kind of Scottish stuff that has lungs in it and gets put into a sheep stomach. That made me think I was going to throw up, and then we saw a plane landing far off that we thought might be Mom's. Nellie and I both said, "Hurry up!" so Uncle Martin did.

After we got inside the airport, we stood a long time watching people come through the doors. I kept asking, "Where's Mom? Where's Mom? When is she coming?" so many times that Nellie told me she wasn't a fortuneteller and to please be quiet. Then Uncle Martin said we should both be quiet because we were in a public place.

Finally we saw Mom. She wasn't wearing her uniform when she got off the plane, just jeans and a puffy coat, so you couldn't tell she was a special person. Except we could, of course, because she's our mother.

She didn't see us at first, but when she did, she waved and ran over. She was crying, which surprised me. Then Nellie cried and I did too, because she and Mom were. And Uncle Martin blew his nose hard and said he was going to check on her bags.

He complained about how heavy they were as we were going back to his car. "Good Lord, Alice," he said. "Have you got gold bricks in here?"

"Just presents, Martin," Mom said. "I brought back some for Lorna Karlsen's mother. Lorna's my roommate; remember? She isn't coming home for the holiday."

"Didn't you bring any for us?" I said.

"Oh," Mom said. "I guess I forgot." Then she smiled and gave Nellie a little wink, but I saw it, and I knew what it meant.

Mom asked Uncle Martin if she could use his car to deliver the presents she'd brought back for her friend. "I don't know, Alice," Uncle Martin said. "It's almost Christmas. Traffic will be very bad."

"I've been driving trucks all over Bosnia, Martin," Mom said. "I think I can handle your car."

So we drove Uncle Martin to the mall to do his Christmas shopping and then Nellie and I went with Mom to do the delivering. Mom said Nellie was allowed to sit in the front seat because of her size, but I still had to sit in the back. We drove out to Morinville, where Lorna's mother lives. It's a different direction than Beaumont and farther away.

On our way to Lorna's house we went past the Major General Griesbach Battalion, which is the name of the army base outside of Edmonton. Just as we got there, we saw a moose munching on some bushes by the road. I don't know if he saw us or not.

Nellie and Mom talked a lot while we were driving. Their voices were very quiet and I couldn't really hear what they were saying, but I could see Mom's face in the mirror and her eyes were sad.

Then when we got back into Edmonton, she suddenly started acting happy again. She asked us, "Now, why doesn't this family have a Christmas tree up yet?"

"Because," Nellie told her, "Uncle Martin made that wire thing with lights on it. He's says *that's* for Christmas."

"Well," Mom said, "that's for *his* Christmas. He's an art teacher. But what about our tree? Haven't we always had one, no matter what?"

"Yes!" I said.

"Okay then," Mom said. "Let's stop by and get one at Super Store. They aren't too expensive there." We got a very nice tree and it was on sale because it was only two days before Christmas Eve. Also we got a string of white lights and a few decorations — some round ones, and some like birds with long, silver tails. They were on sale too.

We didn't get a stand though, so when we got home we had to put the tree in a plastic bucket with rocks around it to hold it still. I thought it was beautiful even if it kept tipping over a little bit.

Uncle Martin came home in a taxicab with a lot of presents. When he saw the tree he yelled, "Oh no! The hardwood! Those needles will be everywhere!"

"No they won't," Nellie said. "We have water in the bucket so the needles won't fall."

"Come on, Martin! Don't be a Grinch," Mom said. "It's Christmas!" Then she gave him a hug and he took his packages and his wire decoration down to the basement.

Christmas Eve was a very good day. When we got up, we had a special breakfast with pancakes and strawberries. Mom cooked it and she made my pancake so it had a little happy face in it. Also she didn't care if I didn't eat any strawberries. She knew I didn't like the seeds.

After that, she showed us some pictures of where she lived in Bosnia. It was like a really small trailer that she and Lorna shared. And we saw her truck that she drives, and a picture of Sherlock sniffing for land mines and one of the school they're fixing up with some kids outside.

But there wasn't a picture of Edin. When I asked about it Mom said he wasn't there the day she brought her camera. She and Nellie and Uncle Martin all looked at each other in a funny way. And then they all stood up and started talking about doing the dishes. They acted excited, like it was going to be a lot of fun.

IN THE AFTERNOON UNCLE MARTIN SAID HE had to get some more groceries, so Mom and Nellie and I went over to say Merry Christmas to Mr. Lapinski. I made a picture frame out of Popsicle sticks at school and painted it bright green. I wanted to give it to him. Also, I wanted Mom to meet him.

Mr. Lapinski was slow coming to the door again, so I used my signal. And I was starting to use it again, but Mom said, "Wait, Lester B. Old people don't move that fast. Give him time."

She was right. In a minute, Mr. Lapinski opened the door. His hands were shaking, but he was all dressed up in a red sweater and a necktie. His hair was combed down too, and he was very smiley. “Mike Hopkins!” he said. “Merry Christmas. And to you too, sister. And Mrs. Soldier Hopkins. Please come in!”

Mom said, “It’s Alice Mackelwain, sir,” and we went into Mr. Lapinski’s house. I gave him my green, Popsicle-stick present which made him very happy.

“Please excuse mess,” he said. “In little while I go to my daughter Magdalene’s for Christmas Eve, so I don’t worry about cleaning up.”

“But your house is always like this,” I said. Mom and Nellie both looked at me and shook their heads. Then everybody sat down.

“You will please excuse me if I don’t offer food to you,” Mr. Lapinski said. “Is fasting day for me until we have dinner tonight. We have lots to eat then.”

Mom told me that fasting means not eating and I asked why.

“Why it means that?” Mr. Lapinski wanted to know. “Or why I do it?”

“Why you aren’t eating, I guess,” I said.

“Is Polish Christmas Eve custom.” Only he didn’t say Christmas Eve. He said something that sounded like the name of a flower and means Christmas Eve in Polish. He made me say it over a bunch of times until I got it right.

All three of us said it actually. Then he told Nellie, "So, Sister. I hear from Mike Hopkins you are very smart. Now Lapinski teaches you to spell this word. W-i-g-i-l-i-a. You can do that?"

Nellie only had to try it twice to get it right. And she didn't act snotty when he called her sister, either. She was very polite.

Mom asked Mr. Lapinski if his family did other Polish things on Christmas Eve. "Not like we used to in Poland," he said. "Then mother cleaned house all day, put up tree late in day. We ate dinner just when first stars were coming out. Lots and lots of dishes. Special bread, fish soup, cabbage. Twelve different things.

"Now Magdalene puts her tree up very early. And we have kielbasa and pierogi. Apple strudel for dessert. All from grocery store. Then we go to midnight mass together."

"Oh," I said. "We just put our tree up yesterday. That's kind of Polish, isn't it?" I looked at Mom. She smiled at me and she even winked. But Mr. Lapinski went right on talking.

"Magdalene still does some things old way," he said. "Always we have white table cloth on table. And we set extra place for mother and brother." He looked at Mom. "They died in war." He never told me that, but I guess I forgot to ask.

"I'm sorry," Mom said.

"Your son," Mr. Lapinski said to Mom. "He reminds me of my little brother Marek." He reached out his hand to me and went, "In Poland, we took leftovers from table and gave to farm animals. Is old Polish belief that on Christmas Eve they speak like humans." He touched my shoulder. "I heard them, when I was boy."

"What were they saying?" I asked him.

"Was pigs who were talking," he said. They asked me, 'Why don't you give us food like this from table every day instead of slop?" He laughed and Mom laughed.

Nellie watched me pretty hard, but I still asked him, "How about the dogs? Didn't you have dogs? And what did they say?"

Mr. Lapinski leaned over toward me. "Only one dog spoke to Lapinski on Wigilia. It was cold night and she was lying in the barn feeding her new pups. I covered her with blanket and she said, 'Bless you, Jozef.'"

"Did she really?" I wanted to know. But Mr. Lapinski just patted my head and gave me five dollars. Then Mom said it was time to go home.

NELLIE WENT BACK HOME, AT LEAST. MOM wanted to take a little walk first so I went with her. First we went to the edge of a ravine not too far from the house. If you stand right on the edge of it you can look out and see down to a little valley with lots of trees, and then the river moving along. It's called the North Saskatchewan. There's a big bridge over it, and even a golf course there.

Then we went part way down some steep steps that start just by the Highlands Senior Citizen Centre. I'm not allowed to go down there alone because people who might hurt me stay there sometimes. But Mom said it was okay if we were together.

We took a little side path through the trees. It was getting dark and we could see the lights of cars crossing the bridge. There were lots of them. Mom told me to look at the moon, so I did. It was really big and yellow and seemed very close. She said, "It looks like there's a face on it, doesn't it?"

I saw what she meant, and I also saw the round holes Nellie was talking about. I knew they really weren't doghouses, but I thought it would be good if they were. I thought it would be good if there was a whole city of round houses, where dogs could live — lost dogs, maybe. Or dogs that had to rest from finding land mines in Bosnia.

That got me thinking about Merit. If she really was dead like I was starting to think. I wanted to talk about it. But I knew I wasn't supposed to bother Mom with things like that, so instead I asked her if she believed in ghosts.

"Like Casper the Friendly, you mean?" she wanted to know.

"Not ones in cartoons," I said. "Real ghosts that aren't mean or anything, but you can still see through them, anyway." We were walking back to Uncle Martin's by then. I was getting very cold, so we were hurrying and our breaths were steaming out of us like we were really fast dragons.

Mom said, "No, I don't believe in ghosts. Why? Has someone been telling you stories?"

"Well," I said. I didn't want to get Mr. Lapinski in trouble, so I told her, "It's just something I thought about. But if animals can talk on Christmas Eve, why can't they come back after they're dead, too?"

"Mr. Lapinski was just telling you a story," Mom said. "I don't think he wanted you to take him seriously."

"He might," I said. Then a car came by slowly and its lights made something shine in the bushes just by Mr. Lapinski's house. It looked almost like two jewellery eyes watching us walk home.

OUR FAMILY DOESN'T DO BIG THINGS ON Christmas Eve like Mr. Lapinski's does. We get up Christmas morning and do everything then. I was awake very early and I tried to get Mom and Nellie interested in waking up, too. But I couldn't. So next I tried Uncle Martin. I went down to the basement where he was sleeping. It was dark and I couldn't find the light switch, but I heard him snoring so I went over to his sound. Also I had a little flashlight and I turned that on.

"Merry Christmas, Uncle Martin!" I said. I did it very nicely, sort of like I was singing. He went on snoring. "Merry Christmas!" I went again a little louder. Then I tap-tapped him on the shoulder and put the light in his face. He did another big snore and then he shook his head and his eyes came open really fast and wide. "What?" he said. "What is it?"

"Merry Christmas," I said again.

So Uncle Martin got up and made some coffee. He said he had to do that first. Then I took some in to Mom where she was sleeping on the floor in the computer room. And she woke up, too. She looked at her watch. "It's 5:30 in the morning, son," she said.

"I know," I said. "Merry Christmas!"

NELLIE HELPED ME GET REALLY NICE CHRISTMAS presents for everybody. I gave my mom some perfume called, "Blue Waltz." It has people dancing on the front and a pretty blue ribbon around the middle of the bottle. Mom put some on her wrists and said how good it smelled. And I gave Nellie some green apple bubble bath. She opened it and said it was like a refrigerator full of apples.

Uncle Martin sniffed the shaving lotion I gave him and then tried really hard to open a window. He twisted his mouth and made a lot of grunting noises, but he couldn't do it. "Frozen shut," he said. He sucked on the finger he just got a cut on and then gave Mom kind of a sorry look.

I also got very nice things from everybody. Mom bought me a game for the computer. Nellie gave me a book called *Dogs that Earn a Living*, about dogs that have jobs like rescuing people who've been buried alive. And Uncle Martin gave me a pair of black skates. I already knew how to skate forward pretty well, but he said he'd show me how to go backwards.

Then Mom said, "Martin. These are figure skates."

"Yes?" he said, like it was a question. Mom looked at him for a minute, and then he said, "He doesn't have to be like everybody else. I have figure skates."

"I know you do," Mom said and kind of shook her head. Then she opened her present from him. It was something very fluffy called a jogging suit. "Pink?" she said, like that was another question. "On someone with hair like mine?"

Uncle Martin said, "Lots of redheads wear pink, Alice. I sometimes wear it myself."

"We've noticed," Nellie snorted.

Mom said, "Thank you, Martin." She put the jacket part over her shoulders and wore it for a while.

LATER IN THE DAY CHRISTINE CAME TO have dinner with us. Uncle Martin is way taller than she is and he had to bend over to give her a kiss under the mistletoe at the front door. It was just a little peck with their lips pooched out but Nellie said, "Oh, brother," and went out to the kitchen. Christine said, "Oh Martin!" in a higher voice than usual. And Uncle Martin made his usual colour change and said, "Oh, Christine, there's a present for you under the tree." Nellie came back in to watch her open it. It was another pink thing, but it had lace on it so she left the room again.

Christine had presents for everybody, mostly chocolates, except she gave Uncle Martin a big box that he said he'd open up later because he had something in the oven. Then he went out into the kitchen and made so much noise banging pans and dropping things and playing loud music that Nellie had to tell him to settle down.

Mom had all the family dishes out on the table with a tablecloth and candles and flowers. And we had gold and silver Christmas crackers with prizes inside them that we pulled open before we ate.

Nellie got a small yo-yo. And Christine got a puzzle game. I don't remember what anyone else got, but mine was little and round and it flew off somewhere we could never find when the cracker popped open.

After that Uncle Martin brought in a big, brown turkey with white, frilly things on its drumsticks. Everyone said, "Ooh!" and "Ah!" There was also mashed potatoes, which I ate, even if they were made from real ones and had lumps. And lots of vegetables and a jiggling red salad that I mostly pushed into with my fork to watch what happened. All the adults had wine to drink and Uncle Martin kept filling up their glasses every time they got empty.

I was hoping we'd have ice cream for dessert, but Uncle Martin brought in a plate of fancy cookies and another one with something long and square on it and a little silver knife beside it. He set that plate down in front of Christine. "For you," he said.

Christine raised her eyebrows like she didn't know what it was. "For me?"

"I'll bet you weren't expecting this," Uncle Martin said. He made his smile go from one ear to the other. "I got the recipe from the internet."

"I'll bet you don't know what it is," Nell said, so I asked, "Do you?"

And Christine said, "I'm afraid I don't."

"But . . . it's from Scotland," Uncle Martin said. I think he was too warm, because he unbuttoned his shirt collar and bobbled his Adam's apple up and down. "Don't you . . . ? It's called Black Bun."

Christine shook her head. "Sorry," she said.

"It's full of nuts and peels and raisins." Uncle Martin counted off all the bad things that were in it. "It's supposed to be a special Scottish dish."

"Oh," Christine said. "Well, we moved to England when I was four." Uncle Martin shot Nellie a look. Then Mom grabbed the dish and cut off a big piece for everybody except me. They all started chewing, which looked like hard work. And swallowing, which didn't look any easier.

After that everyone started on the cookies and Mom asked Christine how she got the kind of job where you pretend to be a dead artist. Christine was using her regular voice again and she said she wasn't always dead. Sometimes she did plays and other things.

"Do you do movies?" I asked her.

She smiled and shook her head. "Not yet," she said.

Uncle Martin sighed, "But she could!" He raised up his glass to her. "She's smart and beautiful. And she could be a movie star!" He was the reddest I've ever seen by then, even redder than he got from eating hot stuff out of the refrigerator. Some hairs were coming loose from his ponytail and he sucked in a few while he was talking and had to spit them out again. Nellie snickered and looked at Mom. Mom snickered and after that everyone laughed out loud for a while.

Then Christine jumped up and started singing *Deck the Halls.* Nellie used to be in the choir in Beaumont, so she started right in and then the rest of us did, even if we only came in on the fa, la, la, la, la part. Christine grabbed up some spoons and started clacking them together on her knee. "If I only had my tap shoes with me," she said. We clapped and made up new verses, and kept on singing until our energy was all used up.

THE DAY AFTER CHRISTMAS IS CALLED BOXING Day, I think because you're supposed to clear up all the boxes from Christmas presents and all the wrapping paper and put it in the recycling. We already did that on Christmas though, so we didn't have any boxing left. But the day after that Mom and Nellie went to a place called Whyte Avenue to have hot chocolate.

It was another women's thing, I guess. Then Uncle Martin said he and I could have a men's day and go skating. It wasn't exactly the same but I said, "Okay," anyway.

We decided to go to Hawrelak Park. After we changed into our black figure skates in the shelter house, we went out on the ice. Some parts had cracks in them from peoples' skate blades, but one part was still smooth and kind of clear so you could see the darkness underneath and the bubbles and leaves that got frozen in. It made me think about drowning, but just for a minute.

We were practising going backwards and I got pretty good. Then Uncle Martin went spinning around by himself for a while. After that he said he'd show me how to balance on one leg, but he tripped and fell so we went into the shelter house to warm up. He was limping a little.

I asked for some hot chocolate because I knew that's what Mom and Nellie were having. While I was waiting for Uncle Martin to bring me some, a boy I didn't know came over. He was bigger than me and he had on an Edmonton Oilers hockey shirt. He asked me, "Are you a girl?"

"No," I said. I thought it was a dumb question since I'm the only boy in my family.

Then he said, "So how come you're wearing girls' skates?"

"Because I got them for a Christmas present from my Uncle Martin," I said.

"From the Sugar Plum Fairy, you mean," he said. He flapped his arms around and pretended to dance on the tips of his skates. Then he walked away. After that I took the black skates off and didn't put them on again.

WHEN WE WERE DRIVING HOME A MAGPIE was picking at something dead beside the road. That got me wondering if all animals had ghosts, like I was deciding Merit did. Then Uncle Martin said, "They're good skates, Mike."

"I know," I said, "but I want to send them to Edin. Mom said he doesn't have any toys."

"What?" Uncle Martin said and he honked the horn to make the magpie fly away. "Edin?"

I said, "The boy in Bosnia who's my same age. The one I sent the shoes to. I'm trying to make friends with him. I think he needs black skates more than I do."

Then we were quiet, but when he stopped for a red light, Uncle Martin watched me out of the corner of his eyes, kind of like Mr. Lapinski did when he was looking at something he wasn't sure was there. "I don't think he does, Mike," he said. "I don't think he has any use for skates at all." He turned on the radio and when the light went green, we started driving again.

I WAS SAD WHEN I WENT TO BED that night because Nellie told me Mom only had two more days before she had to leave again. She said I shouldn't cry about it because we always knew when Mom was going to leave. I cried anyway. And I said I was too sad to have a regular bedtime. But I kept yawning so I still had to have one.

I didn't sleep very long, though, because something woke me up again. I thought it was a dog barking at first because I was dreaming about a black dog who saves people from drowning in the ocean. His name is Ned. There's a story about him in the book Nellie gave me for Christmas.

But it wasn't barking. It was voices. Very loud ones and they were coming from the living room. Uncle Martin's was going blam, blam very low. And I heard Nellie using her settle down voice. Then I heard another voice kind of like crying and it scared me so I got up and went into the hall. Everybody was in the living room. I stopped right at the doorway, but I stayed against the wall so they couldn't tell I was there.

"I don't see why he has to know," Uncle Martin said. "If you tell him now and then leave, there'll be a big problem."

"We can handle it if Mom wants us to," Nellie said. Then she went, "And you both need to keep your voices down or you'll wake him up."

They whispered after that but it was very scratchy whispering like their voices were trying to hurt each other. After a while I heard crying again and Mom said in a very excited voice, "I saw the coffin, Martin! It wasn't any bigger than your coffee table!" Then there was more crying and I knew it was Mom that was doing it. That upset me very much because it was the second time she cried so I hurried right into the room and gave Uncle Martin a very strong look. Then I went, "You stop being mean to my mom!"

Uncle Martin just looked at me. His eyes were red and watery and Mom's were the same way plus she had a lot of crumpled up Kleenexes in her lap.

Nellie said, "I told you so." Then she shook her head and just stared up at the ceiling.

"Son," Mom said. "Martin isn't being mean. It's just . . . " She held out her arms and I went over so she could hold on to me.

"Don't cry," I said. "I was starting to decide she was dead. I've been trying to get used to the idea. But I didn't know about the coffin. Did the lady who buried her get it for her?"

"Her?" Mom went. She moved her head away from me so she could look right at my face.

Then Uncle Martin went, "Her, Mike? What are you talking about?"

"Oh my God," Nellie said. She put her hands in front of her eyes. Then she took them away and looked at Mom. "He's talking about Merit. You think the coffin was for Merit, don't you, Mikey?"

"Well," I said. Everybody was staring at me so it made my stomach very nervous. Also Nellie said I wasn't supposed to talk about Merit to Mom because of upsetting her.

Then Uncle Martin snorted into his handkerchief a few times. "Merit?" he said. "That dog? But she died before you moved in here. That's not who your mother is talking about."

Mom said, "Martin!" She put her flat hand out at him like a stop sign. "I want to talk to my son alone. It's my job to tell him."

So Nellie and Uncle Martin went to bed after that and Mom took me back to my room. She talked to me until I went to sleep, but I didn't really get what she was saying for a long time.

"It's Edin who's dead," she told me. "He and his brother walked into a minefield."

"No, he isn't dead," I said. "We're making friends. And I still have to send him my black skates!" I kept saying that over and over. And Mom kept saying she was sorry. Then I yelled, "You lied to me! You said Bosnia wasn't dangerous anymore!" And I hid away from her, under the covers. I was mad at her for telling a story that wasn't true. For lying.

"It isn't really dangerous where I am in Bosnia," Mom said. "Not if you stay in the cleared areas. But the boys went into a field with red flags all over it. They knew they weren't supposed to. Anyway, Mirsad is all right. He'll need a new leg, but he's all right."

She patted my back but I didn't come out from my hiding place. I stayed there all night. I didn't have any dreams. I didn't see Merit's ghost or Edin's. It was just very black and lonely inside my sleep, and full of shadows.

When I woke up, I knew what my mom had said about Edin was true. It's just that way I have of knowing things. I apologized for hiding. And Mom told me a bunch of times how we'd all be okay. Then in another day or so, she was gone again.

AFTER THE CHRISTMAS HOLIDAYS, MRS. MONTCRIEFF TOLD the class what had happened to Edin. She knew because my mom called her before she left and talked to her about it.

Everybody was very upset. They said, "What will happen to the stuff we sent? What will happen to his brother? How will he get a new leg?"

"Other people can use the things we collected," Mrs. Montcrieff said. She was wiping at her eyes with a Kleenex. "I don't know about your other questions, but Master Corporal Mackelwain will write to us as soon as she knows anything."

A boy named Sheldon who never pays attention asked, "Who's Master Corporal Mackelwain?"

I said, "She's my mother. Don't you remember anything?"

Some people cried when Mrs. Montcrieff told them about Edin. But I didn't. I knew if I started, I wouldn't be able to stop and then Nellie would have come to my school because they always call her. Then I'd feel dumb and sad, so I just cried in my mind like I do sometimes.

MR. LAPINSKI SAID IT WAS A GHOST dog or spirit that helped me when Nellie got attacked. Then Edin died, which wasn't supposed to happen. And Mom went away again and I was mixed up and didn't know what to think. But I was also scared to think that my mom didn't have any help at all, so I kept saying my poem in between my teeth, "Away day, Away day." Then the words started to change and it seemed like I wasn't saying them anymore. Shadows moved around in my head, and the words just came out of my mouth by themselves. After a while they were saying something new. "Run away," they said. "Run away." They said that and said that and lots of times I couldn't get them to stop.

ONE DAY I WENT TO SEE MR. Lapinski after school. I felt nervous of the voice I heard in my head and I wanted to talk to him about it. I thought he wouldn't get mad at me like my sister would.

When I got to his house, I just gave the signal once and then I waited like Mom said to. But he didn't come and he didn't come and I had to wait a long time. Finally the door opened with a kind of whooshing sound and Mr. Lapinski was standing there in his bathrobe.

"Dog Boy," he said. He opened out the glass door for me. Then he went over and lay down on the couch. He had a blanket there and he covered himself with it. The couch is where Denver usually sleeps, but he was on the floor beside the couch. I was surprised about that.

"Are you sick?" I asked Mr. Lapinski, because he looked really pale.

"Just little flu bug, I think," he said. "Denver takes care of me." Denver looked up at me when he heard his name. He thumped his tail on the floor, but he didn't get up.

I thought about how Mr. Lapinski always fed me when I came so I said, "Would you like some cookies? I could get them. We could have cookies together."

Mr. Lapinski shook his head. "Is all right," he said. "I'm not hungry."

"Well," I said. "You always tell me to eat, and now you're getting thin, so maybe you should have a few cookies or something."

"Is true," Mr. Lapinski said. "Pretty soon you can see right through me." He started to laugh and that made him cough.

"My sister could bring you some tomato soup," I said. "If I called her on the phone and asked her I think she would."

But Mr. Lapinski went, "No, no. Don't bother sister. If I don't get better, I call Magdalene." Then he closed his eyes.

He didn't open them again for a long time, so I went, "Okay. I'd better go home now." I was hoping he'd wake up when I said that and tell me to stay. Then he'd get up off the couch for the cookies and we'd eat them and everything would be like before. But he didn't say anything. And even Denver didn't pay any attention to me. He just stayed close to the couch and didn't move.

So I went home. It was almost dark in just the little piece of time I was in Mr. Lapinski's house. Streetlights were coming on and the snow looked shiny and white. Then I saw the jewellery eyes again. They were glittering in the same bush where I saw them before, when Mom and I were coming home from our walk.

I stopped very still when I saw them. I made my hands into fists and I said, "Is that you Merit? Are you a ghost?

Or is it somebody else?" I had to push very hard to get my voice to come out. "And why did Edin have to die? Why didn't you do your job like you're supposed to?" I started to cry while I was talking so when I finished I really needed to blow my nose, but I still stood there waiting and sniffling really hard.

Something came a little way out of the bushes. It was kind of like what I saw the day Nellie got attacked, only brighter now and shimmering like Mr. Lapinski said. It looked at me and I heard it breathing and felt its bright eyes on me. "Who are you?" I whispered. "Where did you come from?"

Inside my head I heard, "Go home now, Mike Hopkins. I'm here to help Lapinski. You're safe. Go home now."

When Mom was back in Bosnia, Nellie started asking me every day if I was okay. "How're you doing, Mikey?" she'd say. Or sometimes, "Is everything okay?"

And I always said, "Fine." Or "Yes," or things like that. But when I went home after visiting Mr. Lapinski I was thinking if she asked me how I was, I'd really tell her. I'd say, "I'm terrible. Voices in my head are telling me to do things. Merit's dead for sure, and Edin didn't get saved. And there's a shimmerdog watching me which no one lets me talk about except Mr. Lapinski. And now he's starting to change!"

But Nellie was busy fixing dinner when I got home because Uncle Martin had a class for adults and wouldn't be home until late. She just said "Hi," when I came in and didn't even look at me, so I went into the bedroom and hid under the covers like I did when Mom first told me about Edin.

After a while Nellie started calling me. Then she came into the room and found me. "Mikey," she said, "it's time for supper pretty soon." But I didn't answer her, so she pulled off the blankets and said, "Come out, Mike. Tell me what's going on."

I didn't like her doing that and I tried to get under the blankets again, but she put her arm over me so I couldn't turn. "Let's talk about it," Nellie said.

Then I hollered, "But you told me I shouldn't talk about it!"

Nellie was quiet. She said, "I know. Mom and I talked and I shouldn't have said that." She took her arm away so I could turn over. "People can change their minds, can't they?" she asked me.

So I told her about Mr. Lapinski, but I didn't say anything about the shimmerdog. And I didn't say anything about the runaway words, either, because I didn't think she'd changed that much.

I WANTED TO VISIT MR. LAPINSKI AFTER SCHOOL the next day to see if he was better. Nellie said just to check if he was all right and not to stay too long, and, "Don't pester him," she said.

"I won't," I told her, because pestering is when you stare very hard at someone or say their name a lot of times, and I never did that to Mr. Lapinski. But he wasn't home. First I just knocked. Then I gave the signal and waited and waited and then gave it again. I did that three times. Finally I went home. "I think he's asleep," I told my sister.

After supper I tried to phone him but he didn't answer.

NELLIE PICKED ME UP AFTER SCHOOL THE next day and we went right home because it got very windy and cold all of a sudden and we were only wearing jean jackets. I called Mr. Lapinski again as soon as I got in the house, and he still wasn't there. Then I went into the computer room to see if we had a letter from Mom. Nellie said as long as she was writing, she was all right.

I was saying my poem over and over while I was waiting for the computer to find if there was a letter. Then I looked out the window and I saw a car pull up in front of Mr. Lapinski's house. It was only four-thirty but it was already dark and the lights from the car made two bright holes in the darkness so you could see how the snow had started coming down really fast.

A lady who looked like Mr. Lapinski's daughter got out of the car and went into his house. I got a bad feeling because he wasn't supposed to be home and she should know that. I stood up and went to get my winter coat but I couldn't find it. Everything was all jumbled up in the hallway — not like when we first came to Uncle Martin's — so I put on my jean jacket again. I couldn't find my boots either, but I grabbed my hat and mitts and scarf. I tried to hurry up but it was like I was inside a place where there wasn't any quickness, so I couldn't.

I know I should have told Nellie where I was going. I know that. But she was in the bathroom fussing with her hair or something, and I needed to go. So I just opened the door and ran across the street to Mr. Lapinski's house.

THE LADY WHO CAME TO THE DOOR was Mr. Lapinski's daughter, like I thought. Her name was Magdalene, but I didn't think I should call her that so I said, "Hello, is your father home yet?" She barely opened up the glass door. She just stayed looking at me and her eyes were like the snowy weather.

"Um," I went. "Well, could I talk to Mr. Lapinski?"

Then she pushed the door open a little bit more. "He's gone," she said. Her eyes and her nose and her mouth all got pulled in together when she said that.

I could tell something was wrong, but I was still full of slowness so I went, "Oh. I know. I've been calling on him." She didn't say anything. "I thought maybe he was sick," I said. "Where did he go? Is he at your house?"

"I'm sorry," Mr. Lapinski's daughter said and then opened the door all the way so that snow started to blow in. "My father is dead."

I just looked at her. I think it was a slow look I gave her, but inside I was starting to speed up like the snow, which was falling faster and faster.

She went, "An ambulance took him to hospital last night, but he died."

Now the shadows in my brain began twisting around like very mad snakes, and it made it hard for me to think. "But," I said. "He didn't tell me good bye."

"Everything happened very fast," she said. "I'm sorry. Please, come in." And I did want to. But I got the runaway voice again, like it was living inside me and the snakes were making my feet move up and down so much I had to start running. I *had* to. There wasn't any slowness left. I was as fast as the wind and the snow. Faster, even. I howled and I shimmered and ran down the street. And then I was gone

I DIDN'T KNOW WHERE I WAS GOING OR anything. I just ran and ran and barked and howled because it felt very bad to stand still. It wasn't like last time, when Nellie was hurt and I saw the shimmerdog, and it said, "Run with me!" Because then we ran together and it showed me where to go.

This time I was alone and all I could hear inside my head was *run away, run away.* So I let me feet do that, but away isn't any place I knew how to find, and there was no one to show me, so I just kept on running and howling.

I wanted to stop. I knew I was still a boy and should quit how I was acting, but I couldn't, even when I got to the ravine. Even when I knew it was dangerous to be there and started running down the steep stairs and went off the path into the bushes, I couldn't stop. Or when I fell and hurt myself. I scratched my face and lost my mitts, but my legs still wouldn't let me quit. And the words wouldn't, either.

Then I put my hand in my pocket and found the dog rock. It was still there from Nellie's bleeding day. I pressed my hand around it very hard, and just after that, I found a cave in the bushes and I went in. Then everything quit all at once. The words. My legs. Everything except the wind and the snow.

I FOUND PART OF AN OLD BLANKET IN the cave. It was thin and rough, with lots of holes, and it had a sad smell, but I put it around me anyway.

After that I started shivering. Or maybe I started before that, but it was very bad shivering, anyway, like my arms and legs were trying to get away from the rest of my body. I didn't whine or whimper or make any more dog sounds, but I did cry like I did when I was little and I wanted to see my dad. I kept wondering how long it would be before my mom found me. After a while I tucked my head down in the blanket and closed my eyes like I was dead again.

Then, all of a sudden, I felt someone watching me and I looked out of the cave. Something big was there. It stood outside the cave looking in at me with bright eyes, and it glowed like it was made out of snowflakes with moonlight on them. I wasn't afraid, because I knew it was the shimmerdog and I was very glad.

Very slowly he came inside the cave and filled it all with brightness. First he said something I didn't understand. Then he told me, "You're safe now." And he walked over to me on big, quiet paws and curled around me. I got warm and toasty and my arms and legs stopped shivering. Then I went to sleep. That's what I was still doing in the morning when Mr. Lapinski waded through the snow and found me.

I DIDN'T KNOW IT WAS MR. LAPINSKI AT first, of course, because I was sleepy and I wasn't really expecting him. Then he said, "Who's this?" kind of in Mr. Lapinski's voice.

And I went, "I'm Mike Hopkins."

"Mike Hopkins!" he said. "I've been looking for you. What are you doing here?"

"My legs started running and got me lost," I said.

"This is a dangerous place for a boy," he told me.

"I didn't mean to be here." I said. "But your daughter said you were gone and wouldn't be back. And then my legs wouldn't stay still." I didn't want to use the 'd' word because of how it would make him feel, but I asked him, "Are you back to stay now?"

Mr. Lapinski laughed and said, “Everything comes back, Mike. Don’t they teach you that in school?” A dog barked then, but it was like laughing, too.

Mr. Lapinski picked me up in his very strong arms. That’s when I noticed he wasn’t wearing his glasses any more. And when I looked right at his eyes, I could tell that he saw me.

The dog came over beside him and it was strange because it was little now. And it wasn’t exactly white anymore. “Why did you change?” I asked the dog from inside my head where all my words were, but then I went back to sleep and didn’t hear the answer.

How Everything Comes Back

NELLIE SHOWED ME WHAT IT SAID ABOUT me in the Edmonton Journal. It said, "An eight-year-old boy ran away from home last night in the snow storm and stayed alone in the ravine all night." Then it went, "The boy's mother is in Bosnia doing a peacekeeping mission."

There was other stuff about how a homeless man named Joseph found me and took me to the Highlands Senior Citizen Centre. A nurse said, "It's very lucky Joseph found the little boy. He's a kind man who often comes to the centre with his dog this time of year to get warm and have a bowl of soup. When the uncle came by looking for his nephew, Joseph went out looking too."

It wasn't a homeless man who helped me, though. That wasn't right. It was Mr. Lapinski. Or maybe it was his ghost. I can't decide about that. And our shimmerdog was there, too. I wanted to tell people that. If I could have said what really happened, I would have.

WHEN I WOKE UP AT THE CENTRE, a nurse kept asking me who I was and where I'd been and I tried to tell her, but the shadows wanted me to keep my mouth closed and I couldn't do anything about it. They hardly even wanted me to eat.

Then the police came and I couldn't tell them either. But they knew my name some way and so Nellie and Uncle Martin got to find out where I was. They came and got me and took me home.

Nellie kept saying, "Mikey, I was so worried about you. Why didn't you tell me where you were going?" Sometimes she looked very mad. And sometimes she cried. But mostly she sat with me and told me things. Like she told me how Uncle Martin yelled when he called Bosnia and told them it was an emergency and he had to talk to my mom. And he kept calling and calling. Once he pounded his hand down on the table and said a swear word.

Finally he got Mom on the phone and she said she was coming home as soon as she could. They let you do that if you're a peacekeeper and something very terrible is happening to your family.

But even when Nellie told me that Mom was coming home soon, I still couldn't say anything back to her.

I SLEPT A LOT THE NEXT DAYS AFTER my legs got me lost. At first, Mr. Lapinski came to visit me. He still had his new eyes and they were easy to look at. He talked to me every time he came, and mostly it didn't make sense. But what I remember is, "Only listen to the good voices, Mike Hopkins. They will never hurt you."

The big white dog was with him too. In the beginning it shined so bright it made my eyes watery, but every time it came it got smaller. It never talked in my head again, but once a hollow moonbeam bubble came out of its mouth with a little, tiny dog inside. I held out my hand, but it floated up into the ceiling and disappeared.

After a while, Mr. Lapinski got harder to see and he stopped trying to talk to me. He just sat on the bed beside me and patted my hand.

Then Mom got back. And once when I was sitting on her lap I looked over her shoulder and patches of him were there in the hallway, watching us and smiling. The dog was still with him, too. Then they faded away and I never saw them again.

AFTER A WHILE, MOM AND UNCLE MARTIN and Nellie had a big argument. I think he forgot that I could still hear, even if I wasn't talking, because I was only in the next room and I heard him say in a loud voice, "Well, he can't just sit here like a vegetable not talking! He needs to see a doctor. They have drugs for this kind of thing."

"No!" is all Mom said, but she was very loud when she said it.

"Alice," Uncle Martin said, "we can't go on like this."

Then Nellie blurted, "I thought drugs were supposed to be bad for kids. That's what they tell us at school."

After Uncle Martin left and slammed the door, Mom and Nellie came into the bedroom where I was. "Sorry for the shouting," Mom said. "It's very hard with all of us living in the same house."

And Nellie said, "Sorry for upsetting Uncle Martin, Mom. But he comes up with such clueless ideas."

Then when Uncle Martin came back Christine was with him. She asked me how I was in a cheerful way, and gave me a little stuffed dog. And Uncle Martin said he was sorry for the name calling. He went, "I don't really think you're a vegetable, Mike. You don't even eat them." I think he was making a joke.

Anyway, everybody was sorry. I wanted to say I was too, but the 'S' and the 'O' got caught in my throat and wouldn't let the other letters come out.

A GOOD THING HAPPENED AFTER THAT, THOUGH. THERE's a place on the army base that helps families. Mom went there and got the name of someone called Dr. Penny Li. She's retired now which means she doesn't work to get paid, but only if she wants to.

Dr. Penny doesn't give needles or anything like that. She mostly tells stories or sometimes does art with you. Right away I liked her because of her name and because she has bright, crinkly eyes like the birds that come to Uncle Martin's feeder in the winter. She's also kind of small like them, so when she started visiting me in the afternoons I felt very tall.

Dr. Penny told me good stories, like one about a boy who took all the bad things in the world inside him until it made him feel so full he had to move out of his body and live on the ceiling. He stayed up there a long time until he learned how to let the bad things out one at a time.

She asked me interesting questions that I wanted to answer some day if the shadows ever let my mouth start working again. Also, she let me paint and draw and make things out of modelling clay.

At first I only liked to paint with black, but then I started adding colours. First it was just white and silver. The day I put green in, Dr. Penny asked me, "When Mr. Lapinski found you in the ravine, did he say anything to you?"

And I took the black pen I had in my hand and I wrote, "It's dangerous here." I probably didn't spell it right, but she knew what I meant.

Dr. Penny nodded. "Anything else?"

So I wrote, "Everything comes back." Then I smiled because I was so glad that my hands were talking, even if my mouth didn't want to do its job.

ALMOST EVERY DAY AFTER THAT, I WROTE in a red book that Dr. Penny gave me. I put in as much as I could about what happened, even if it took a long time to get it down. Then she asked me questions about my writing and I wrote back to her some more.

Dr. Penny was very interested to hear how the dog brought me back after I drowned. And about Mr. Lapinski and his brother in the war. She told me, "Everybody has important jobs to do in their life, Mike. Maybe one of yours is remembering."

I tried to draw the white dog but I'm not a very good artist, so it was mostly white squiggly lines on dark paper. But I guess you don't have to be good at art to put your feelings down that way because Dr. Penny liked my drawing. She put it in a folder and she wrote on it in slanty letters, *Mike's Visitors.*

MOM ASKED IF SHE COULD SEE MY book. At first I wasn't sure I should let her, because of what I promised Nellie. But Dr. Penny said, "It's okay, Mike. Your mother can handle it."

Mom cried while she read it, which I was getting used to. But she said she liked it. And she told me she wanted to know everything I felt like telling her from now on.

ONE SATURDAY IN THE SPRING MOM WENT out to the army base to talk to some people. And Nellie went to a girl named Priscilla's house to do homework, which left me and Uncle Martin at home doing jobs. First, we uncovered the picnic table and got the chairs out of the garden shed.

Then we opened up the green and white sun umbrella and stuck it through the hole in the middle of the table. After that, Uncle Martin gave me a spray bottle of cleaning stuff and a rag and told me to start washing off the furniture while he raked the flowerbed.

But I found eight ladybug beetles crawling on the inside of the umbrella who I think had spent the whole winter there. And I was more interested in them than in cleaning. Uncle Martin was just starting to remind me to get to work when we heard a loud clanging noise coming closer and closer. He stopped talking and turned his head really fast like someone was yanking on it. "I wish she'd get that fixed," he said, just as Christine stopped her car in the alley. She jumped out and ran over to us. She didn't even close her car door.

"Hello, boys," she said. She never used that high, silly voice any more, but Uncle Martin still got rosy every time she gave him a smooch on the lips.

Then she came over to me and tugged on my arm. Christine cleans houses when she doesn't have dead people jobs or plays to do and I think she was supposed to be working then because she was wearing her pink T-shirt that says *Tidy Team* on it. "Come on, Mike," she said. "We need to hurry." I shook my head because I had three more ladybugs to find a safe place for.

"I just saw your dog, Mike," Christine said. "We need to hurry."

UNCLE MARTIN DECIDED WE SHOULD TAKE HIS car because Christine's was too noisy and dangerous. Then he decided to go with us because Christine might be a dangerous driver as well.

"I hope you know what you're doing," he told her after we were on our way.

"I do," she said. Then she turned around to look at me and went, "I was vacuuming and dusting at this big house. I had the TV on for company — it was the show where they bring in an animal to see if someone will adopt it. And there she was. Your dog was on TV!" That got me dizzy in my stomach.

"Someone left her out in the country," Christine told me. "She had porcupine quills around her mouth so she couldn't eat or drink water. And Mike?" I shook my head because I didn't want to hear what she might be getting ready to say. "They say she's had pups, but something happened to them." She undid her seat belt and stretched her arm out to touch my hand. "It will be all right," she said in her nicest voice. "She just needs you to take her home."

UNCLE MARTIN DROVE US TO THE EDMONTON SPCA, which is a place where they take animals that people don't want or they're being mean to. I was afraid to go inside because of what I might see, but Christine held my hand and Uncle Martin even held the other one.

When we got in, we heard dogs barking and cats meowing and a parrot squawking on top of everything. Christine asked the man at the desk if we could see the TV dog. "She isn't back from the station yet," he said. "But it shouldn't be too long. We're already getting calls about her."

Uncle Martin wanted to go back home but Christine said, "No, we're waiting." So we sat outside on a bench. While we were there a man walked by with a little boy who was crying and carrying a cat in his arms. When they came out again, the cat was gone. Then a woman brought in some kittens. She had them in a box but they kept meowing and reaching their paws out over the top.

Finally, a dark blue van pulled up with *SPCA* in white letters on the side and a man and a dog got out. The dog wasn't on a leash but it still waited on the sidewalk while the man took something off the back seat. Then he patted the dog's head and they started walking to the building together.

"There's your dog, Mike," Christine said. Then she got up and started talking to the man. "Martin? Mike?" she said, so Uncle Martin and I got up, too.

AT FIRST, I DIDN'T BELIEVE WHAT CHRISTINE said was true, because Merit was white and the TV dog was kind of a sandy colour. Also her tail and ears were different. But I really wanted her to be Merit, so I stood up and had a good, long look. And after that I looked some more. I saw the scabs around her mouth where porcupine quills used to be. And I saw the feeding places on her stomach that her dead puppies were supposed to drink from.

Finally, I knew it was her. The moonbeam bubble came back then. I couldn't see it because it was in my stomach, but I felt it glowing there. It squeezed up through my throat and right into my mouth. This time there was a word inside and when the bubble popped, the word pushed out my mouth and into the air. I sighed when it came out and there was moon dust on my voice, but she heard me anyway. "Merit?" I said. And she was shy but she licked my hand.

Everybody was nice to me when I finally went back to school. It was just for a few mornings right before summer vacation. Mom was starting her new job driving a bus that takes people in wheel chairs to places they need to go, so she picked me up at noon and took me home. Then after Nellie got back from school, Mom went out driving again.

But she was doing good things even before that. While I was still feeling very bad and quiet, she went to visit kids at my school and other ones, too. She told them about Edin and about how Mirsad, his brother, needs to get a new leg which will be very expensive because he'll have to go away to get it. And more than once too because he's still growing. Then he'll have to learn how to walk on it.

Lots of kids wrote letters to people like the Rotary. That is a club of men that have money to do good things for people. I wrote, too and I think they're going to help Mirsad. I think we might even bring him to Edmonton to get fixed up at the University Hospital.

That's the end of what I have to say. Except in the summer we moved to an apartment in the neighbourhood. Mom said she and Uncle Martin got along better when they didn't see each other every day. Also Merit was with us again, so we were all tired of hearing about the hardwood floors being scratched. Even Christine was. She was at Uncle Martin's a lot by then and she told him, "It's only something to walk on."

Dr. Penny still came to talk to me and sometimes to my whole family. When fall came, she said I could try going back to school all day for a while, and then we'd see. It was hard, but it mostly worked. Merit was used to her new body and to being back with us again so she picked me up from school and walked me home the way she used to. Nellie liked that especially because she was very busy at JAWS and didn't have time to pick me up every day. She and her friend Sam started something called SAVE, which means "Students against Violence Everywhere". I think they were going to call it "Students Together against Bullying," but when they just used the letters it came out to be STAB which they didn't like.

Anyway, things are almost back to the way they used to be. But not quite. When Mr. Lapinski told me how everything comes back, he forgot to say that when it gets here, it can really be changed.

DIANNE LINDEN's first novel, *Peacekeepers* (2004) was shortlisted for the R. Ross Annette Award for Children's Literature (Alberta Writers' Guild), and the Red Maple Young Readers Choice Award. She is co-editor of the anthology *Running Barefoot: Women Write the Land*. Her essays have appeared in Canadian, British and American anthologies. Dianne Linden lives in Edmonton, Alberta.